Room For One More

A 3-4-1 Collection

Stories and Poems by

Christine Ricketts

Nicole DeGennaro

Kaitlyn Sudol

Lara Eckener

With Art by

Alex Griggs

Katie Lee Grosskopf

Rebecca Wilcox

Room For One More: A 3-4-1 Collection

This book contains works of fiction. All names, characters, places, and events are either products of the authors' imaginations, or are used fictitiously. Any resemblance to actual events, locales, or persons—living or dead—is entirely coincidental.

Published by: 3-4-1 Publications

ISBN-13: 978-0-578-77573-9

Cover layout by Carly Schnur

To Mom and Jess

- Christine

*To everyone standing up for
justice and equal rights:
Keep fighting the good fight.*

-Nicole

Table of Contents

About the Authors...VII

About the Artists..IX

Acknowledgements...XI

Introduction..XIII

Part I: Myth

    The Long Way Around 4

    Allure of Choice 21

    And Echo 33

    Tardy 38

Part II: Folklore

    The Hag's Hand 48

    You May Yet Find Them Blind 69

    Across the River 72

    The Woods 88

Part III: Oracle

    Elegy for Spent Sweat 97

    Damned if You Do 102

    That Which Should Become 122

    Hydrophilia 127

Part IV: Urban Legend

    The Hitchhiker 136

    Best Laid Plans 148

    The Last Ride 153

    In the Air 166

Behind the Tales..167

About the Authors

Christine Ricketts has been writing for as long as she can remember and boy, are her hands tired. She also enjoys reading, playing video games and theoretical attempts at organization. On rare occasions she will do something involving that so-called "reality" people are always talking about. She doesn't really see the appeal.

Christine provided the art for "The Long Way Around", "The Woods", "That Which Should Become", and "Best Laid Plans".

Nicole DeGennaro is a human being who exists. Sometimes. When she isn't toiling over the written word, she is often wasting time on the Internet or annoying her cats. She also takes on way too many projects for her own good, but she enjoys all of them. You can learn more about all that at her virtual Batcave: *http://nicoledegennaro.wordpress.com/*.

Lara Eckener loves to collage with both words and pictures. You can find her words and art at *LaraEckener.com*. You can find more of her words in *Drawn to Marvel: Poems from the Comic Books, Strange Romance Volume 2, Undercities: An Anthology from Dirty Birds Press,* and *Paper & Kindling: A 3-4-1 Collection.*

Kaitlyn Sudol is an aspiring children's author with a boring day job. She lives in the Boston area where she spends a lot of time having brunch and talking about horror movies, comic books, musical theatre, and kidlit. When she's not reading, writing, or brunching, she's probably recording an episode of The Worst Bestsellers or mindlessly refreshing the internet. You can hear her complain about the MBTA at @*fourteenacross* on Twitter or hear her talk about literature of questionable quality at *www.worstbestsellers.com*.

About the Artists

Rebecca Wilcox is a writer and illustrator who is entirely too fond of coffee and fountain pens. Her science fantasy novel *The Savage Way* was selected as a **RevPit 2020** winner. When she's not dreaming up space operas and alien beings, she's busy raising two daughters who love giant robots as much as they love sparkly ponies. She currently lives in central Florida with her family and an assortment of cats and small fish. Rebecca can be found on Twitter and Instagram *@Wilcox_RL*.

Rebecca provided the art for "And Echo", "In the Air", "Elegy for Spent Sweat", and "You May Yet Find Them Blind."

Katie Lee Grosskopf is a Portland Oregon-based illustrator and designer, where her love of animals, moderate temperatures, independent bookstores, powerlifting, museums, and abundant vegan food options truly thrives. More of her work can be found at *www.seekatiedraw.com*.

Katie provided the art for "Across the River", "Tardy", "Damned If You Do", and "The Hitchhiker."

Alex Griggs is a graphic designer living in Seattle, Washington. She finds her days most happily enjoyed when they have involved soccer, beer, and cats.

Alex provided the art for "The Hag's Hand", "Allure of Choice", "Hydro-philia", and "The Last Ride."

ACKNOWLEDGEMENTS

Christine would like to thank Nicole, Kait, and Lara for agreeing to this
project. She really feels like she's pulled the wool over their eyes twice now.
Thanks also to Katie, Alex, and Rebecca for the phenomal art. Also thanks to
Sangsook Pak for catching our grammar errors, Tara O'Hare for her very
helpful inDesign advice, Carly Schnur for laying out the cover, and Megan
Buckman for some awesome epub skills.

Nicole would like to thank her friends—old and new—and her family
for always supporting her writing. She would especially like to thank her
Tuesday Night Zoom hangout group for helping to keep her grounded during
2020 and giving her a place to vent or play Animal Crossing for hours on end
with no judgment. She is eternally grateful to Sangsook Pak for making the
time even in this hellish year to copy edit these stories; they are better thanks
to your discerning eye. To the artists and other writers in this collection:
thank you for contributing your creativity to this endeavor. I know at times
it was a challenge to feel creative with everything going on in the world, and
I'm glad we completed this labor of love together.

Lara would like to thank Alli Martin, Jessica Scott, Nanci Schwartz, Brian
Larsen, Sarah Bay, Paloma Rohrbaugh, Kaitlyn Sudol, Nicole DeGennaro,
Christine Ricketts, and many others for their unending belief and support.
She would also like to thank Lisa Thomas for holding on to that pesky soul
for her.

Kaitlyn would like to thank her fellow writers and artists for the work they
put into some truly incredible pieces, Christine specifically for managing,
wrangling, and organizing this collection, the late, great Alvin Schwartz for
providing kids everywhere with an introduction to the spectres of American
folklore, and the more contemporary work of Colin Dickey, for giving her a
nudge to think more critically about those spectres.

Introduction

I can't exactly remember how old I was when I first took an interest in mythology. There are three moments that I can recall that vie for the title of *Thing That Got Me Hooked*. First, I read in my school reading comprehension text book the Greek myth of Deucalion and Pyrrha, which directly led to me stealing my sister's copy of *Cliff Notes: Mythology*. (Which, apparently, she stole from someone else because that is definitely not her name scribbled on the front page. Whoops.) Second, for twenty-five cents, my Nanny bought me a copy of *The Eight Days of Luke* by Dianne Wynne Jones from a garage sale, a wonderful introduction to Norse mythology. (I only note that it was twenty-five cents because the little sticker is still on the book some thirty years later.) And thirdly, my brother borrowed the computer game *Hero's Quest: So You Want to Be a Hero* from his friend in which the fantastic character of Baba Yaga plays a key role. (Her house has chicken legs! Why? Just. Why?)

Thus began my fascination with mythology. I'm sure that scholars would argue that some things that I label as mythology really should be classified as folk tales or legends or other things. (Actually, I know this for a fact based on the Great Courses Great Mythologies of the World course, but since that professor said I could lump them all together, that's what I'm doing.) To me they all have one very important thing in common; they deal with unexplainable things. They have an otherness about them, they look past logic and reason and tell the stories that live there, where things don't make sense and they don't have to. (A house! With chicken legs!)

So for this volume of *3-4-1,* I thought, what better avenue to explore than mythology? A genre whose very genetic code involves retelling and reimaging, from the simple shift from Greek to Roman where we mostly swap names of gods and goddess, to oral traditions where nearly everything changes with every telling, to Russian tales where everyone is named Ivan and houses stand on chicken legs. (Reader, I have read a lot of Eastern European myths. They never explain the chicken legs. And I would just like a chicken leg origin story.)

If you haven't read any of the other collections, then here's what we did: each author wrote a story based on a myth, legend, or folktale. Then, we all read those stories, found something in them that we loved or that inspired us, and wrote a kind of response story or poem. Sometimes the inspiration will be very obvious. Sometimes it won't.

To go along with each story and poem, we brought in some tremendously talented artists to provide an illustration and each artist played a similar game of finding inspiration. They are truly stunning pieces and I'm so thrilled with the visual accompaniments to the wonderful works of words that you'll find within this book.

I invite you to join us on this journey through an eclectic mythos; there's always room for one more!

- Christine Ricketts

PART I

Myth
a traditional story, especially one concerning the early history of a people or explaining some natural or social phenomenon, and typically involving supernatural beings or events.

The Long Way Around

Christine Ricketts

It wasn't that Owen was ignoring the clock. In fact, his eyes kept flickering over to it as if a constant line of sight could somehow stop the steady progression of the little hand. He knew exactly what time it was and exactly what time he was supposed to have been somewhere else and exactly how far apart those two instances were quickly becoming.

On the other hand, despite his constant checking, the time on the clock didn't really mean anything, not when compared to the measure he was twisting and tweaking on the paper in front of him.

"You're going to be late." Her voice was an airy mixture of amusement and reprimand that served as a stark contrast to the heavy bass tones that were rhythmically sounding in his head.

Late was exactly what he was trying *not* to be, but then she probably wasn't talking about the—"I'm always late."

"Yes. And it's not nearly as charming as you think it is."

The notes in his head shifted, the heavier sounds falling back as lighter tones took their place, like shy creatures coaxed forward by the pleasing timbre of her voice. He followed the movement with his pen, chasing the melody as it formed; he could find the time later. "Luckily, Phil employs me for my fantastic showmanship and musical diversity, not my charms."

She smiled at him, a wry and exasperated curve of her lips that threatened to steal his attention. And if he had any beats or seconds to spare, he would have let it be stolen. But as his time was already compromised—

"You don't think he wants that showmanship and talent at his bar when his customers are?"

Owen squinted, his nose inches away from the sheet music he was scratching notes onto.

"I just want to get these notes down before I forget," he replied, pausing when the ink in his pen ran dry. He shook it fiercely and then scribbled on the corner of the sheet until he had coaxed it back to life; he only needed it for a few more lines.

"You never forget notes," she called back, her voice fading. In one ear he could hear her shuffling in the next room, gathering together the bits and pieces she needed for her own work. He didn't need to watch her to know exactly where she went; she kept everything in the same spot.

In the other ear he heard the delicate tune that he was scribbling down, its progression far lovelier than his messy, barely legible scrawl. Not that it mattered. She was right; he never did forget a note.

"What time do you think you'll be home?" she asked, leaning around the empty doorway, both of her hands engaged in twisting her long brown hair back and up in a complicated maneuver that she somehow made seem effortless. He tossed his pen down onto the sheet music and stood, reaching over to grab the sturdy violin case from off of the floor where he'd carefully packed it before the music had caught his focus. When he turned back, he saw that she'd picked up the pen and snapped the cap firmly into place.

"This is why your pens never have any ink left in them," she pointed out, tossing it back onto the pile.

"Without you, I'd have no music to write and nothing to write it with," he quipped, catching her around the waist and pressing their cheeks together. Hers was smooth and soft against the rough stubble that he'd forgotten to shave off that morning. She laughed and patted the side of his face.

"You'd also be colossally late, instead of just marginally."

Grinning, he pressed a kiss to her cheek and released his hold.

"I should be back by eleven. I'll stay an extra fifteen to make up for being late."

She fluttered her eyes at him. "Your responsibility makes me swoon," she teased.

With one hand on the door, he raised his fingers to his lips and blew another kiss.

"I love you."

"I love you, too."

He walked the same way to work every day; three blocks down from their apartment, a right, three more blocks, a left, another couple of blocks and a bridge that spanned the smallest body of water to ever be called a river and then straight on to Phil's Brewhouse. And while Neverland may not have been the final destination, it was a simple route that didn't require a car, and except on days when it rained or snowed it suited him just fine.

The most interesting aspect of the entire walk was the bridge; it was made of stones of oddly uniform greyish cast, fitted almost perfectly together. Set dead in the center was a tunnel to let the water pass through to wherever it was that it passed on to.

It was a very nice bridge.

Still, each day that he crossed over it he could not help but wonder why anyone had bothered to build it. The river was not very deep; it must have taken more effort to put the bridge up than it would have taken to just fill in or dry out the barely moving water. More puzzling was the fact that the bridge had been built into the side of a hill; why hadn't they just put the road over the hill?

It had been there for as long as he knew and had that worn, weathered look that really old buildings had, like the ones built when people used horses to get around. Maybe the river had been more impressive back then. Maybe wherever the tunnel let out had once been an important meeting spot (he imagined it probably led into a drainage system now). Maybe locals had loaded up boats and traveled downstream to trade.

The idea made him smile and whistle a few bars of *15 Miles on the Erie Canal*.

When he reached the middle of the bridge, he paused and glanced over the side. The river looked almost the same as it did every other day with low, barely moving, muddy water and absolutely no ripples or bubbles to suggest anything was swimming below the surface. (He'd tried to imagine what kind of creature would willingly make a home in that particular environment and had stopped when his imagination had come up with a multi-eyed alien that had creeped him out.)

Something was different, though; an addition that he had never seen before. Just a dozen or so feet away, floating lazily toward the bridge, was a simple wooden dinghy. Inside lay a young woman, her eyes closed. As far as he could tell, the boat seemed to be empty of anything else—no blanket, no bag, not even any oars.

Owen leaned over the side of the bridge, looking for any hint that she was aware of the fact she was drifting closer to the tunnel's entrance. Unease began to crawl its way down his spine. He assumed that waking up in a drainage sewer was not how she had envisioned her afternoon.

"Uh, Miss? Miss, I think . . . hey, can you hear me?"

The boat continued its quiet journey forward. He hurried to the opposite end of the bridge and picked his way down the shallow embankment to the water's edge. By then, the dinghy was near the mouth of the tunnel, and he had only a couple of seconds to decide if he was really planning on wading into a stream after a sleeping young woman who might be perfectly fine.

The front of the dinghy slipped out of sight. A moment later he was plunging into the water and sinking immediately up to his thighs. *This is going to be a fun story to tell,* he thought as he struggled forward. At the last second he recalled his violin case strapped to his back and lifted it up over his head with one hand.

The unexpected depth of the water slowed him, and he did not catch up to the boat until it was already well inside the tunnel.

"Excuse me, Miss," he said, stumbling as the water level rose abruptly from his thighs to his stomach. Owen grabbed hold of the stern and pulled himself up into the boat, trying his best not to rock or drip too much. "Miss?" he tried again.

In the rapidly fading light he could see she looked paler than she had from atop the bridge. Her hair was golden, as shiny as the coin resting over her closed lips.

"What the . . ." he murmured, ducking down to look closer. The boat jerked forward abruptly, and he had the sense that it was moving much, *much* faster than before. He turned back to look over his shoulder, but the entrance to the tunnel was growing smaller, suddenly further away than he would have thought possible.

He wondered if now was the time to abandon ship, so to speak. Maybe he could try and pull it back—

"I wouldn't if I were you. Not many people survive two dips in the sticks."

The calm, silvery voice gave him such a start that he nearly pitched over the side. He assumed that the sleeping woman had finally awoken to her— well now *their*—predicament and thought that was rather odd advice to hand out to a complete stranger.

"You'll have to give me a minute. It's been a while since I've had one of you along, and it can be a bit tricky if you're not careful," the voice continued, as if Owen had any idea what it was talking about. It was difficult to tell exactly where the melodious sound was coming from, but something in the words made him think that it was *not* the lady that was speaking to him.

But before he could respond, a blast of stunningly cold wind rushed over his face, stinging his skin. Even as his eyes watered and the tips of his ears burned it was followed by a soothingly warm breeze.

"You might want to close your eyes," the voice recommended, just as a blindingly white light exploded, filling his vision with a starburst of colors before he clamped his eyes shut. His stomach dropped and they were falling and then suddenly not. There was a heavy *sploosh*, like the sound of a rock dropped into a still lake.

He had a feeling that they might have been the rock.

"You can open your eyes now. Shouldn't be too bright for you."

When he did so, the tunnel and the light had both been replaced by a muted grey mist that stretched in all directions and drifted just above water as still and smooth as glass. Not even the passage of the boat disturbed the glossy surface. Out of the corner of his eye, he saw a flap of something dark; he twisted toward the front of the boat and watched a tall, thin man lean down over the body of the woman. Before Owen could protest, the young man plucked the coin from her lips. He held it up between his index finger and thumb, then brought it to his own mouth, setting it between his teeth and biting down. Inspecting it, the young man appeared satisfied and slipped it into a simple leather pouch that hung from his neck. Then he turned to Owen with eyes that were deep and annoyed.

"I won't even bother asking for your fare. Your kind never bothers to bring any," he declared with a rather put upon expression, leaning on a pole that Owen was rather certain hadn't been there a moment before and which trailed through the water beside the boat, also without leaving a wake.

Owen blinked. "My kind . . . fare, what . . . who the hell—" he looked around—"where the—" he looked down at the girl, as still as the water they drifted upon—"Is she—" he looked back up at the young man—"Who are you?" he finally spit out.

The young man held his arms out, perched on the air as if he were in a chair.

"Who do I look like? The ferryman, of course," he replied as if it were the only possible answer. "Who are you? No, never mind. I suppose that doesn't really matter, does it? Who is it that you're looking for?"

"Looking for?" Owen echoed.

The ferryman bobbed his head—reminding Owen a bit of a teenager listening to headphones—and peered out over the water as if looking for a landmark. "No one comes down here unless they've reason to be here. Since you're not here to stay, you must have come for someone. A lover? A child? I won't bother telling you that you can't take them. Your kind never listens to *that* either."

Owen shook his head, feeling as if there were vital pieces of information that he was missing concerning the whole situation, some understanding that would make the previous and current events sensical. The young man, or ferryman, in front of him certainly seemed completely at ease, as if transporting two complete strangers from a dark tunnel into a water-filled twilight was an everyday occurrence. Well, he *was* a ferryman. Owen looked closer at the young man and *young* suddenly seemed like the wrong word to use. Not that he appeared old or anything. His face was smooth and unlined, and his features were firm and well defined without the pull or sag of age. But there was something around the eyes, something other than just annoyance. . .

Maybe he'd tripped and hit his head on his way to work. Or maybe he'd never even got out of bed that morning; it certainly wasn't the strangest dream he had ever had.

"I just saw her, floating toward the tunnel and I thought—I thought she might need help."

The ferryman looked down briefly and patted the pouch around his neck.

"No, she had all the help she needed. It's rather surprising for these days actually. Quite surprising."

Something clicked in Owen's mind. A river. A ferryman. A coin on the lips. Not sticks. *Styx.* He'd heard a story like this before, and it didn't involve an eighties rock band. He relaxed slightly. *Definitely* a dream.

"She's not sleeping, is she?" was what he said.

Tugging idly on one earlobe in a strangely unexpected gesture, the ferryman shook his head, his attention still directed out over the water.

"Oh no. Well, that is, not in the same way that you mean."

Owen felt strangely calm. *'Where are we?'* had an answer, albeit a rather odd one. He didn't think that cruises to the Underworld were particularly common. He glanced down at the young woman. Then again, maybe they just weren't widely advertised.

"It's not far now. There's a road that will take you back to where you came from, though you may be later than you'd like, especially if you stray and doubly so if you visit," the ferryman continued.

"What?"

"Roads are strange. They can lead to journeys and journeys can take you many places, some you don't mean to go to and others you'd rather not. Give me a boat any time."

"A boat is how I got here in the first place," Owen pointed out.

"That's not the boat's fault," the ferryman countered.

Owen didn't think that made much sense but it seemed rude to say.

Up ahead the fog slowly parted, and a shore of white sand appeared. Two boulders of solid black stood next to one another, like a giant open doorway. Between them ran a well-defined path leading off into a forest. An ordinary forest in the middle of a vast body of water navigated by a tall, thin man that took coins off of dead people.

If it was a dream, he wondered what the psychological meaning behind all of that was.

If it wasn't a dream . . . he tried to think of a story he knew where the person walking into the forest *didn't* end up in a bad way.

The boat bumped gently into the sand. Owen looked to the ferryman, who motioned with his chin toward the path. On unsteady legs, Owen pulled himself out of the boat and stepped onto the shore. His feet sank into the sand.

"Take this road all the way to the end and don't step away from it." There was a lilt to the ferryman's voice that made Owen look back again. "You will anyway, your kind never can help it, but try not to wander too far for too long."

The ferryman straightened against his staff, moving as if to push off from the bank.

"Wait!"

The ferryman paused and Owen fished into the right pocket of his jacket, pulling out the old harmonica he occasionally used in performances. He raised it to his lips and blew a slow succession of notes, like a sketch of the droll ferryman. He built the melody quietly until he had what felt like a fitting tribute to the odd fellow. Then he let the final note ring out, where it echoed across the waters.

"In lieu of a proper fare?" he offered, tucking the instrument away. It wasn't the first time he bartered a song for a service, but it certainly was the strangest supper of his life. The ferryman sighed and pushed off from the shore.

"Music may fill a home but it hardly fills a coffer," he quipped, tapping the coin purse again. As the boat drifted backward though he pursed his lips and began to whistle a fair approximation of the tune. Owen figured that was as good as any handshake.

He turned to the path. The shore and water faded off in either direction, like canvas for a painting that hadn't yet been filled in.

"Don't take too long!" The ferryman's voice carried back from where he and the boat had disappeared into the fog.

"Or what?" Owen called back.

"Or you'll be late."

"For what?"

"For everything."

Owen began walking. The path was simple; just packed dirt that ran between clusters of narrow, white-trunked trees. Twilight twisted amongst them as silently as it had drifted over the water. He tried peering deeper into the forest as he passed, but there was nothing to see besides grey mist. It made him think of late evenings after heavy snowfall when it was too dark to see and sound had been muffled by the cold. In those moments, music had always seemed to drain from him; he'd never been compelled to break those winter silences.

But now he could hear the echoing dirge-like tones of the tune he was thinking of as *An Ode to the Ferryman*.

It took him a minute to realize that he was hearing the notes of another melody as well, one being played outside his mind.

He paused in mid-step and held a hand up to his ear. The pitched sounds of a flute came from off to his right, a string of joyous notes he recognized immediately. He'd heard it an innumerable amount of times and ways, through tinny sounding earbuds, blasted by car stereos, crackled out of an old record player. Without a second thought he stepped off the path, sliding between two slender trees as he went. The twilight gave way instantly to a bright clearing where a grey-bearded man sat atop a moss-covered boulder, playing a simple reed pipe. A chorus of laughter cut off, and Owen had the sense of someone or something departing, though there was no one else that he could see.

The older man continued to play, eyes closed and unaware of the change in his audience. Owen reached him at the same time that he blew the last note of his melody. He opened his eyes and gave a small start upon seeing Owen there.

"Oh, hello there."

"Hi. You're Grey Morris." There was no question of it. Owen knew that face better than some of his own relatives, and he had never even *met* the man. It had stared back at him from dozens of album covers and carefully sought out music magazine articles.

"I am. Or, I guess I was." The older man scratched at his beard and frowned slightly. "Not sure how that works now. Though if I'm supposed to be someone else, I guess they would have told me that."

"This is incredible. I'm a huge admirer of your work. It and you have always been a huge inspiration of mine. I always hoped that I'd get to see you play. I actually was there at your last performance but . . . ." Owen trailed off, not sure how to finish when he realized what was waiting at the end of the sentence.

Grey looked amused. "But then I croaked backstage, didn't I?" He patted his chest, wide and deep beneath a simple dark t-shirt. "Old ticker gave out. Probably should have taken a bit better care of it but there you are."

Owen looked around at the sunlight-drenched clearing with amazement. "So, I guess this is heaven? You just sit in a beautiful spot and play music all day?"

Grey shrugged and rubbed a hand over the back of his head. "Suppose so. I just got here a few minutes before you."

Owen blinked. "But you died almost six months ago."

"Has it been that long?" Grey scratched at his chin again. "Seems like hardly a moment or two. Actually, I don't really recall how I got here. There was a tall fellow in a boat, grumbled something about a fare. Then there was a pretty lady; she didn't say anything. And then I was here. Where did you come from?"

"There's a road," Owen motioned over his shoulder, though he could no longer see the path he had been traveling on. "I'm supposed to take it all the way to the end. I heard your music and, I mean, how many chances like this was I going to get?"

Grey nodded and, squinting slightly, pointed a finger toward the case on Owen's back.

"Well, if you've no other pressing engagements and you know how to play that fiddle you've got on your back, maybe you'd like to join me for a song or two?"

Owen was already pulling the violin off of his shoulder before the offer was fully made.

"I'd be honored."

When Owen left the clearing, he found himself back on the path, right where he had left, though the twilight had deepened, edging closer to the blue-black of night. He hardly noticed; the songs he had played with his idol—Grey Morris!—hummed in his head, butting up against his *Ode* and weaving into something completely new. Something haunting but lively, sad but with joy as well.

If he was dreaming, he seriously hoped he could remember it when he woke up.

The sound of barking interrupted the joyous symphony in his ears. A moment later a stout black and tan beagle wiggled out of the bushes on the edge of the path, its white-tipped tail wagging frantically.

Owen stopped and stared, feeling his stomach clench; there had to be a million dogs just like it. He'd seen a pair of them just the other day on his way to work. Phil had one; sometimes he brought the old boy to the bar where it would flop down in the corner and snooze. It didn't have to be—

"Boots?" he called out. The dog gave two cheerful yips and bolted back into the forest. Without hesitating, Owen followed. Beneath his feet the path twisted; one moment he was stepping on dirt and the next he was stepping through another pair of trees into yet another forest, this one caught in the midst of fall. Brightly colored leaves swayed on the branches surrounding him. Boots appeared again, rustling between his legs. Owen reached down and rubbed his hands through the dog's soft fur, feeling wetness on his cheeks. He stroked the dog's broad head and wondered how he'd break the news to his dad, or if his dad already knew.

A *swishing* sound filled his ears, and though it could have been anything, with Boots lapping at his face, he knew. He stepped around a pair of leaning elm trees and knew who would be standing behind them before he even saw her. It hurt; his throat closed up tight and his chest ached. Six years later and he still wasn't over losing her.

Dressed in a white turtleneck under an old denim shirt and jeans, his mother stood with a rake in her hands, carefully sweeping leaves into a tidy pile. Her hair was a halo of gold in a setting sun, and she looked healthy and vibrant, the way he always tried to remember her.

She turned and caught sight of him. One hand lifted to her throat. "Owen."

"Hi, Mom," he managed. She smiled, the same wide, happy smile she had always given him. "I'm just visiting," he added quickly and saw the relief as it rushed over her face.

"How exactly did you manage 'just visiting'?"

"I was trying to be helpful."

"Hmm, heard that one before."

They both laughed but it faded quickly, in a way it never had when she had been alive. He looked at her, and with a painful jolt he realized that he had done what he had thought he never would. He'd forgotten. Just little things, like how she stood and how she moved; exactly what her voice sounded like and how much he missed her. There were days when he didn't think of her at all.

He stared, his throat filled with a mixture of sorrow and happiness that was difficult to swallow. His heart was screaming to wrap her up in a hug but his mind wasn't sure he could bear to let her go. He'd never wanted to let her go but she had. She'd gone so fast.

"There were a lot of things I wanted to say to you before . . .things that I didn't get to," he fumbled, swallowing. She reached out and patted his arm gently; the familiar gesture further tightened his throat.

"Like what?"

He thought for a long moment, going back to the last few weeks of her life, back to when he had been convincing himself that she still had time, that he still had time, that things couldn't have been so bad, not with her, not when he could still hear the smile in her voice even over the phone.

He shrugged and shook his head. "I love you. I wanted to tell you that," he said finally.

She gave his arm a squeeze. "Oh, you did honey. You always did." She smiled and he finally saw the tears that she had never shown before. "How's Erin?"

"Good, she's really good."

"You still planning on getting married?"

"Yeah. Sometime next year. I wish you were going to be there."

"So do I. You set a date?"

"Not yet but we've still got time."

"Never as much as you hope," she mused. Before he could respond, she squeezed his arm again. "You better get going or you won't have any at all. Now, give me a hug."

When he tucked his face into her shoulder and felt her arms squeeze his waist, he thought, *I remember this. I'll always remember this.*

When he exited the forest, darkness had fallen, and he could barely see the path in front of him. Pale greenish lights hovered on either side and back among the trees, but he found that he had no desire to investigate them. There was a chill in the air that had not been there before, and it snatched at the warmth of his skin. Owen tucked his arms across his chest and lowered his eyes to the road, determined to make no more stops.

He had not managed to go far when he saw another light up along the side of the path, this one burning the warm, bright orange of flame. A young boy with curly hair dancing along ruddy cheeks stood holding a simple brass lantern.

"I don't suppose that you have another one of those that you'd be willing to lend?" Owen asked the boy when he drew close enough to not be shouting. The darkness did not seem the place for raised voices. The boy smiled and held the lantern out to him.

"No need. You can have this one."

"What about you? Won't you need one?" he inquired, accepting the lantern.

"I see well enough without it."

"So. Do you just hang around here waiting to hand out lanterns?"

The boy laughed, a sound much lower and older than expected. "Oh no. I'm a messenger. I've come to tell you that you're late. If you don't make it through the woods by morning, you'll miss her altogether."

"Miss who?"

The boy continued as if Owen hadn't spoken, pointing down the path. Owen looked but saw only more darkness. "Keep going, and no more stopping for chats."

When Owen turned back, the boy was gone. He stared at the place where the boy had stood. And then slowly the notes of the song he'd been traveling with fell together in his mind. Ice formed in his stomach. Holding the lantern aloft, he began to run.

He couldn't say how long he ran—his breath seized painfully in his chest, but his feet were light. The darkness gradually gave way faster than he would have thought possible. He came to the end of the path just as the night faded into the muted grey of pre-dawn. The path ended at a shoreline nearly identical to the one he had been left upon. Guiding another simple rowboat to rest against the sand was the same tall, thin ferryman. In the boat was another woman, and though the face was too far away for him to see, he was sure that he knew who it was.

"Erin!" he shouted.

For a long moment nothing happened; it was as if the stillness had swallowed his voice only a few feet from his lips. Not even the ferryman raised his head in greeting.

But then the woman in the boat sat up, her back to him. She began to turn, and just as he was about to see her face, she was gone.

He was in a tunnel, like the one at the start of his journey only there was no river and no boat. Just a long corridor of darkness and at the end, far in the distance, the faint light of an opening.

"You can't get to her going that way."

Owen started to spin around but a firm pressure on his shoulder prevented him. He thought it was a hand, could feel the individual grip of each finger, but when he looked down, there was nothing.

"Don't look back. Look forward."

His eyes snapped up, back to the small point of light. It seemed closer now.

"Tell me how to get to her," he begged quietly, not even trying to hide the desperation that he felt.

"What would you do if you could get to her?"

"Take her back," he replied.

"But life doesn't go backward. It goes forward."

He frowned. "This isn't life."

"Isn't it? Everyone and everything dies; you are aware of that. Your idol. Your childhood pet. Your mother. All in time."

"Then what does it matter if she comes back with me? We'll both be back eventually. I know there's no escaping it."

"Does this seem like a prison to you? Did you see any boulders being pushed up hills or food and water denied? Do you see bars or cages or chains?"

He flinched at the sudden, quiet anger. "No, but—"

"Do you think this was a place created *for* you? To house you like collected artifacts? To snatch you from the arms of life, like babes from the arms of mothers?"

"I love her."

"Do you think that changes anything? You can't go back. Only forward."

He felt his own rage wash from him until only grief remained.

"Please," he could not help but beg again, having no other words left.

There was silence. And then a sigh that filled the tunnel like a rush of wind, stirring the air and echoing along the walls.

"Each time they come it's always the same, my love."

There was another pause and then, "Would you play your music? It has been a long time since there were any in these halls."

Owen slowly pulled the violin from his shoulder, its weight a burden like it had never been before. He opened the case to the violin, searching his mind for a song that would suit. But all those that he could recall felt forced and false. Taking a deep breath, he set the instrument beneath his chin. Closing his eyes, he set the bow against the strings and played from his heart instead. He played, the notes trickling up from his chest, out through his hands and back into his ears, carrying with them a whisper that echoed in his mind.

"There was another who journeyed here to save his love; I will offer you what we gave to him. Lead your love back to your world but do not look back at her until you have crossed the boundary between them, or else she will return here."

When he opened his eyes, he felt a presence behind him and started to turn, catching himself at the last moment.

"Erin?" he asked instead. There was a quiet rustle and then,

"Owen? Is that—where have you been?" Her voice sounded strange; distant and weak. The acoustics of the tunnel or perhaps the oddness of hearing without seeing. She felt further away than another room, though he could feel the press of her against his back.

"I got . . .sidetracked." Owen chuckled and shook his head. "It's been pretty crazy actually. Let's get out of here. I'll tell you about it later." He began to walk, his ears tilted back as much as he dared. After a moment, he heard the scrape of her footsteps following.

"Where are we . . . we looked everywhere for you."

The walls of the tunnel lit up suddenly, flickering like a projector. Moving images appeared soon after, a silent movie of events he had never seen.

Erin standing with arms crossed in front of her chest, concern radiating from her face as she spoke hurriedly to a police officer.

A missing person's poster, his image and details printed out on it.

Friends gathered around a cemetery, Erin dressed in the black she always hated to wear, his father standing beside her looking far older than he should have. Owen's name carved into a granite stone, a birth date and a question mark below.

He frowned and turned his gaze from the walls, looking down at his feet.

Boxes strewn around their apartment, gradually being filled by Erin and others, some that he recognized and some that he did not.

Erin somewhere, in some unfamiliar space with an unfamiliar man and

something akin to a smile on her once always smiling face.

Owen closed his eyes but the images continued, running across the inside of his eyelids.

A wedding. A delivery room. A holiday party with a mixture of friends and strangers, his dad holding a beer and talking animatedly with the unfamiliar man while two children raced about.

Scene after scene flickered by until finally there was only Erin, much, much older, lying asleep in a bed, her chest barely rising and falling, rising and falling, ceasing to rise. He opened his eyes; the pictures faded from the walls, and up ahead he could see the exit, the light as bright as at the end of any tunnel.

"You can't come with me, can you?" He barely heard himself whisper the words and wondered if he truly had.

"I had a life. It wasn't the one I expected, but it was a good one. I learned so much about how to move forward. I don't think it would be right for me to go back."

"What about me?"

There was a long stretch of silence. And then, "Well, you still have your fantastic showmanship and musical diversity."

The bark of laughter took him by surprise, even more so when he realized it was coming from him. It worked through him, mixing with sadness until he was shaking uncontrollably in a weave of cresting emotions, much like the melody he had played only minutes before.

He turned slowly, before he could stop himself, knowing that he would only have a glimpse. Her face was older, riddled with the lines of all the years he missed. But the blue eyes were the same, and so was the smile that graced her lips.

And then she was gone, and he was falling backward through the exit of the tunnel, enveloped by the white light.

He sat at a bar, a bottle of water and a glass of pale beer in front of him. His break was almost over; he was due back on the small stage in five minutes. Or maybe his set was already over and he was moments away from leaving for the night. It was hard to keep track of the beats and measures now; they would start and stop, dragging him in circles like a song stuck in his head until he was dizzy and had to rely on the bartender to remind him of the time. He looked up, and the woman behind the taps pointed to the clock and then to the stage.

Owen took a sip of the beer and felt a movement just to the left of him. Turning his head, he saw a young man, clean shaven with dark hair. Upon being noticed, the young man smiled so enthusiastically that Owen couldn't help but offer his own smile in return.

"I just wanted to tell you that I love your music. My boyfriend and I come here all the time to hear you play. Your songs are so diverse, and your stage presence is amazing."

Owen wanted to laugh; he might have, only he wasn't sure if the words had been spoken or if he was just hearing their echo in his head. Instead he nodded and shook the young man's hand. It was large and slightly rough but still somehow reminded him of her.

"That last song you played reminded me of Grey Morris' *Off the Water*. You ever hear that song?"

The rhythm in his head paused and the notes that had been following it crashed together; Owen blinked.

"Yeah, actually. That song was sort of a twist on *Off the Water*," he said, fumbling a bit with the words. He blinked again at the young man. "You listen to Grey Morris?"

The young man shrugged and shook his head. "My parents were really big into him actually. They said they liked the way he made everything sound beautiful and that they always enjoyed things more when he was playing in the background. Interpret that as you will."

Owen wasn't sure he could.

"But I sort of get what they meant I guess," the young man continued. "Like, when I hear you play I get this sort of rush of feeling, like I'm going to burst with happiness or sadness or whatever you're playing. It's really cool."

There was something he could say to that, something he wanted to . . .

"Thank you," Owen said after a moment. He looked down at his beer, watching the tiny bubbles burst near the top. He nodded. "Thank you," he said again.

Then he stood, and stepped back towards the stage.

ALLURE OF CHOICE

Nicole DeGennaro

Had another one today," Grey calls across the clearing. "Wasn't expecting so many."

For a few moments—or perhaps longer; time is hard to track in the underworld—the whispering rustle of a breeze in the trees is the only reply. Grey begins to meander through a gentle melody on his flute.

In the middle of a phrase, a young woman with a curly fauxhawk crowning her head steps into the clearing. Her bright red crop top is an odd spring flower against the browns and greens of her forest surroundings. She stays just at the edge of the tree line until he finishes playing, only approaching once his final note has faded.

"They're like weeds," she says, as if she knows she made him think of flowers. "They just keep popping up."

He rests his flute in his lap. "I don't mind it, exactly. I just didn't think this place was so easy to find." She's told him her name before, but he's forgotten it. He finds it's hard to keep new information in his head, although everything from his life is clear as cool water. But he suspects she doesn't remember his name, either.

"It isn't," she shoots back. She sits down on a rock a few feet away from the tree stump on which he sits. Everything in the clearing has a certain familiarity to it, an inviting sense of wear. There, a patch of dirt as if thousands of feet have worn away the grass. Where he sits, the stump is curved as if it has served as a seat longer than it was ever a tree. It's like his favorite small town bar venue, with creaky floors and crooked stools—not exactly home but comforting all the same.

"How do they find it, then?" He's not expecting her to have an answer, but without the minor details of living to create small talk from, like weather and vacations, it's easier to talk about what's on his mind. "Maybe they want to see someone they miss. Maybe their longing leads them here."

She shifts, going from a cross-legged to a straight-legged position. Her brown skin has a golden glow to it, as if it's reflecting a sunset he can't see. She bites her bottom lip, giving his question more consideration than it really deserves; it either has no answer or many answers.

"Maybe," she says, but in a tone that really means *I don't think so.* "But if that were true, I think we'd have more visitors. The living have a lot of longing."

Grey nods. She's got a lot of wisdom for someone likely half his age. Although in the afterlife, age doesn't really mean anything. For all he knows, she's been here for hundreds of years, and if that's the case, then he's the young one.

"So why can't everyone find it?"

She laughs, but in a good-natured way that sounds like an instrument only she can play.

"Grey, if we knew that, I think everything would make a lot more sense."

Shit. She does remember his name.

"I just don't get it," she says one day as she bursts into the clearing, more like a storm than a flower. It occurs to Grey that he never goes to visit her. Either he starts a conversation with the expectation that eventually she'll reply, or she comes by when she wants to talk.

"What's that?" He should just ask her name again, but now that he knows she knows his, it seems rude.

"I mean, they're told to stay on the path, right?" Instead of sitting on the rock as usual, she's pacing near the trees, gesticulating in the direction of said path. Even in her agitation, Grey feels more—well, *alive* wouldn't be the correct word given their surroundings, but *present*. He's more aware of the movement of the leaves, the singing of the birds, the sweet scent of fresh grass.

Grey nods in response to her question. Does her name end with an A? No, an E.

"So...why don't they stay on the path?"

"I mean, how often do you do what you're told?" he counters.

She stops pacing and turns to him with a grin. "No one tells me what to do anymore."

"Okay, well. When you were alive."

She purses her lips, the grin turning into a slight frown, and he knows he got her.

"Point taken. But if you were accidentally somewhere you shouldn't be, wouldn't you follow directions intended to help you get home?"

Now she's got him. She resumes her pacing as he thinks her question over; each time she turns, the tip of her steel-toed boot digs into the ground, tearing some of the grass. She's looking at the sky—well, he thinks of it as the sky, but it isn't really. There's light, maybe even real sunlight. It certainly feels like it. But when he glances up, it's just a gray-white haze.

Does her name start with a P? No, he doesn't think so.

"I mean, the ferryman tells them," she bursts out, now gazing out into the woods. "He *tells them*. Stay on the path, or you'll be late. But then they find someone here they *have* to talk to. And it always comes out that we think we've been here a lot less time than we have."

She taps her temple with a finger. "Can't they put two and two together? Why would time work the same way for the living and the dead?" Grey can't remember ever seeing her this agitated before.

"The ferryman *could* be more explicit," he says.

She waves that excuse away like a gnat.

"He's hardly human; he thinks he's being very direct." She has her back to him, and she picks at a leaf on one of the trees. The grass has already regrown where she had destroyed it with her pacing. The tree is the same; Grey can barely see the moment she pulls a piece of the leaf off because it is replaced in almost the same instant. These small details snare his attention until he loses track of the conversation. He shifts on the stump so he's comfortable again.

"Hey," he says. *God* if only he could remember her name. "What's bothering you?"

She freezes. "Nothing. Never mind." Without looking back at him, she walks off into the trees. Despite her red shirt, he loses sight of her quickly, as if she too were a blemish needing to be covered.

He doesn't see her again for a while. It takes him a day or two to notice— or what passes for days here. Instead, other neighbors come to visit: an older blind fellow who just likes to sit and listen to Grey play; a middle-aged blond woman who sometimes comes by with her dog. He can't remember their names either, but he's more confident that they also don't remember his, so he doesn't feel so bad.

They don't have the same restless energy as the young woman, although they're both pleasant company in their own ways. Still, there's a difference between them and her, the same way there's a difference between her and Grey. He can't quite pinpoint what it is, but he's more aware of it when the woman with the dog or the blind man is around because they remind him of himself in a way the young woman never does. Maybe it's that they've all been here a similar amount of time and the young woman has been here longer—Grey is almost certain of that, the more he considers it, although he doesn't know where that certainty comes from. Something about how she moves through the space or interacts with it, with a familiarity that only forms over an extended amount of time.

"Have you met our other neighbor?" Grey asks the blind man one day, after he finishes playing a short, cheerful ditty. It had dawned on him that sometimes the man talks about the woman and her dog, and vice versa, but neither of them ever mentions the young woman.

"She's a younger woman, doesn't really stay still," he adds, but then comes up at a loss for how else to describe her that doesn't sound just plain weird.

"Yeah, I've met her," the other man says after a time, frowning. Grey stifles a relieved sigh. "I wasn't sure she was real, to be honest."

"How so?" Grey asks, although he just as easily could have said *I know what you mean.*

The man is silent for a long time, running a hand back and forth over his salt and pepper buzz cut as if trying to shake something loose.

"Everything feels different when she's around." His voice is soft, uncertain. Grey understands that, too.

For a moment he considers asking if the fellow remembers her name, but somehow that feels like cheating. Then, before he can say anything, the man speaks again.

"I don't think she belongs here." He's dropped his hand to his lap, where now one thumb runs over and over the knuckles of his other hand. One of his legs is also jiggling up and down. His obvious nervousness sends a chill through Grey; at a loss for any other response, he chuckles.

"She belongs here as much as the rest of us."

The man doesn't reply; Grey isn't sure he actually heard him. He's fallen still, which is somehow more unsettling than all his fidgeting.

"Could you play something?" the man asks after a long silence. "Something happy."

His voice sounds distant. Grey lifts his flute and begins to play. The man stands up and wanders off before he finishes.

"Are you there?" he asks, keeping his voice low. He's walking the perimeter of the clearing, trying to peer through the trees for any flash of red fabric. One of the infuriating things about how time works—or doesn't—in the underworld is that he doesn't know if he should be worried or not. Maybe she's only been gone a couple of days. Or maybe it's been years.

After walking around a few times, occasionally calling out to see if she'll hear him and come over, he stops at the spot where she usually emerges. There's no reason to worry—everyone here is already dead, so what danger could befall them? She probably visits a lot of different people and just hasn't circled back to him yet. He comes up with a few more excuses, then inhales deep and takes a step into the woods.

"Are you Grey Morris?" someone asks from behind him. He freezes. "I can't believe this. I'm a huge fan!" For the first time, he's annoyed to have a living visitor. Why do they think he has nothing better to do? That they can barge in on him just because he's dead? It was a rare fan who would be entitled enough to try and sneak backstage to see him when he was living, yet here they have no such boundaries. He can't see the path from his clearing, and he wasn't even playing—how did this person find him?

"One and the same," he says as he turns back. It's a young man; most of his living visitors are. Are they the only ones bold enough to come down here with oxygen still in their lungs, the only ones confident enough to think they'll make it back to the surface? Or are they the only ones foolish enough to ignore the ferryman's advice and wander off the path?

He motions the young man forward, his initial annoyance fading. Technically he does have all the time in the world, so why shouldn't the young man assume he could spare some?

"I remember my dad playing your songs for me…" and the young man is off. Grey tries to listen, he really does. He's usually not this ungrateful. He usually likes to hear their stories about how they found his music, how much it means to them. It's what he loves most about music, his own and others', that each piece tells someone a slightly different story.

But all he can think about when he looks at the young man is how much of his own time he's wasting just to speak to Grey.

". . .play with you?" the young man finishes, glancing at him and then away. Grey's broken heart is breaking again. How will he feel if Grey says no? What will he be missing if Grey says yes?

He tries to explain this to the young man, the tradeoff he's making without knowing it, but the words keep dying in his throat. The young man looks back at him, hopeful, while Grey flounders.

How often do you do what you're told?

Grey stifles a sigh. He supposes the ferryman is the only one who can warn them, since safe passage is his job. Even if he could get the words out, it would seem like an excuse, a way to deny his request without giving an outright refusal. And the young man has already spent time with Grey that he won't regain when he returns to the surface. So he picks up his flute and smiles at the young man.

"Of course."

The young man beams and pulls the guitar from where it was hanging across his back. As they begin, Grey wonders for the first time if he is actually in hell.

"You should have said no."

Grey startles to attention, although he didn't realize his mind had wandered. He looks up and grins when he sees her tawny eyes. He's relieved, even if she looks annoyed.

"I know," he says as she approaches, and her eyebrows arch in surprise. "Haven't seen you in a while; where have you been?" It sounds more accusatory than he intends.

"Around," she says with a shrug. "Sometimes I...need more space, I guess." She sits on the grass next to him, bringing her knees to her chest. For the first time he thinks she's as young as she looks. "Why didn't you say no, then?"

"I don't know. I wanted to." Grey sighs. "But then I thought about how crushed he would be if I said no, how he'd carry that with him the rest of his life. Which would be worse? Losing a year to play with me, or having that extra year of disappointment to live through?"

She has a distant look in her eyes; her fingers are picking at the frayed ends of her cutoff shorts, worrying away strings of the denim. Those, too, reappear at the same time she peels them off. An infinite thread.

"I didn't think I'd have to worry about anything down here," she says. "But maybe worrying is just what I do." Something about it knocks the wind out of Grey; it's the first time she's really spoken about herself. He wonders how she died. Maybe she already told him and he forgot.

"We can't tell the living what to do," he says; he means it literally, from having attempted it with his most recent visitor, but also in a more figurative sense. Because nobody understands the internal logic of someone else, and even two people who make the same choice make it for different reasons.

"It doesn't mean I have to enjoy watching them make poor decisions."

She's still somewhere else, her eyes unfocused. He lets the silence linger, spending the time trying to remember her name. It's become more than a challenge; it's become a key, something he's certain will unlock his understanding of her.

When the birds start chirping, he wonders if they're dead too. They must be. Or maybe they found their way in and got stuck, like at an airport terminal. Although he supposes they wouldn't have anything to eat down here. Is everything dead, even the trees that still have green leaves? Is the illusion of sunlight created from beams that once shone on the surface?

"That part's no different than being alive," he says finally, and that brings her back. She turns to look at him. He hopes for a half smile, but it doesn't appear. "I guess we can never escape bad decisions—our own or someone else's."

She laughs; a short, stifled thing that's gone before he can appreciate it. "And here I thought I was the pessimistic one," she says.

"But...the bad decisions are the ones that make things interesting, you know," he continues, although now he's mostly just talking for the sake of talking. He isn't usually one of those people, but right now the silence is a looming thing that he'll do anything to keep away. "If we all only made the right decisions, there wouldn't be much life to live." She scoffs.

"That's such a load of shit," she says, to his surprise.

"For a pessimist, that seems pretty optimistic."

"So someone who makes the best choices, they can have less of a life than someone who makes the worst decisions possible? You don't see how that glorifies ignorance and suffering?" Without intending to, he sparked something within her. She unfolds herself, rises to her feet, begins pacing.

"*And* it discounts the fact that sometimes you're in a situation not by your own choice—or that sometimes the choices you have are all bad," she continues, talking more to herself than to him. There's a comfort in knowing that even though they've disagreed, he's managed to bring her back from wherever her thoughts had taken her earlier.

"How you deal with *that* is the interesting part." She comes to a stop in front of him. "*That's* the living in life. And that's the torture of being here." Her skin is glowing in the spectral sunlight that haunts the underworld.

He looks up at her, sensing some kind of expectation, and he knows he'll let her down. Because he isn't understanding what she means.

"I'm . . . sorry, I—"

"—don't worry about it. I'm just rambling," she says, absolving him. Just like that, she has distanced herself again.

He stands up, but she's already gone back through the trees. A feeling creeps over him, a certainty he never had about anything when alive. She's been here much longer than him, maybe much longer than anyone else. What she's trying to put into words are the parts of this place the light doesn't touch, that the visitors don't see, that even the inhabitants won't find unless they spend their infinite time looking.

Grey clutches his flute, but for the first time he can remember, he doesn't feel like playing.

She hasn't reappeared, but their last conversation has lingered. He hasn't played a note since she left. If he's ever slept while here, he hasn't lately. He's been aware of every moment passing, trying to solve her riddle without her help, because he can't think about anything else. It has occurred to him, more than once, that it is not something to be solved, that maybe it is just something to drive him insane, to make him second-guess this pleasant afterlife.

Is it being here that's torture, or is it *thinking* about being here that's torture? After all, he was perfectly happy with this place until he started examining it. Then it started to look more like a trap than a paradise. Not for the dead, but for the living. How do they *find* him, all these fans that drop in to play or talk? He must be one of billions or trillions of people here, if everyone ends up here when they die. So how do they find *him*? Do they have to want it bad enough? Does a part of them not want to return to their life? But they all seem so surprised when they stumble across him.

The odds of that being a coincidence are too astronomical for Grey to fathom.

With these thoughts cycling through his head, he steps into the trees, the same direction that she usually comes from. He has to see what's beyond this clearing. Eventually he'll find a field, or maybe a stream, or even the path that the living are not supposed to stray from. He'll find *something* that smothers the scream trying to climb out of his throat. *Anything*.

But it's just forest. He's pushing through branches and stumbling over his own feet, and the trees just keep going and going and going, crowding in around him, clutching at him with their spindly claws, until it's just a wall of bark, trunks so thick he can barely squeeze between them and so tall he can't see the gray-white haze of the sky.

Instead of feeling soothed, his heart is stammering in a way that would be alarming if he weren't already dead. Reminding himself he doesn't really need to breathe anymore should help, but instead it only makes his chest tighter. The air is heavy and stagnant, suffocating him.

He tries to squeeze between two trunks but can't quite make it, chipping bark off the trees. It grows back in an instant, digging into his skin again. It takes him a moment longer than he'd like to pull himself free; out of spite he rips off more bark, but even as he holds it in his hand, it reappears on the trunk.

Everything in this place is *just so*. The clearing with its worn patches of ground, its comfortable stumps and rocks. But it never gets worn down to the point of looking shabby, or overgrown to the point of looking wild.

His body spasms; the bark in his hands falls to the ground. He understands now, and he wishes more than anything he could return to ignorance.

Maybe . . . maybe if he goes back to the clearing he can start over, forget. He spins on his heels, prepared to retrace his steps.

But he's already there, standing right at the edge like he never left. The trees are their usual height and girth, letting in the gray-white haze of the sky. The dead birds are singing their usual songs.

And she's there, her red crop top vivid as a bloodstain. She's holding his flute, looking it over with tears in her eyes.

"Stefanie. . ." he whispers; her name coming to him out of nowhere, like it followed him back from the forest.

She holds the flute out and approaches him.

"You really should stay here, Grey," she says. She stops when the flute is within his reach, but he doesn't take it. She doesn't move, either.

Nothing about her is menacing—in fact, she's several inches shorter than him when they're both standing. Her posture is relaxed, her eyes wide in a question: *Are you OK?*

No, he isn't. But he doesn't know if that's her fault or his.

He reaches up and takes the flute, holding it close to his chest, hoping it can slow his stammering heart. Then he eases himself onto the stump. He looks around, expecting something to be different. But it's all the same. It all looks the same. Why doesn't it feel the same?

"Why . . . why do I have to stay here?" he asks, his voice hoarse. He never sounded that bad when he was alive, not even when he was smoking a pack a day before he got his big break. Stefanie stays where she's standing; can she tell that everything is different?

"Because it's where you need to be." She answers as if it's another one of their normal conversations. Is this how everything they've discussed has felt to her? Monumental? Terrifying? She tilts her head so she meets his eyes, her expression solemn.

"Why didn't you just say—" his tongue sticks to the roof of his mouth, so he swallows and starts again. "Why didn't you just say it was a trap?"

"Because sometimes it isn't." She pauses with a frown. "Or maybe it always is but sometimes it doesn't matter."

"Stop!" he shouts, although he's pretty sure she was done. "Stop talking in riddles."

Stefanie gives him a confused look. "I'm speaking as plainly as I can. Some things are as hard to put into words here as they are up there."

He's still clutching his flute to his chest, he realizes. He tries to put it down, to relax, but his fingers don't uncurl. His arm doesn't move.

"Is this . . . are we in Hell?" he whispers and closes his eyes, as if that will lessen the impact of her answer. Stefanie sighs. The birds keep singing. She approaches, her footsteps gentle like a doe's, and then she puts a hand on his shoulder.

"It's complicated," she says. "Being dead is no more simple than being alive."

When she withdraws her hand, he opens his eyes and looks up at her. She opens her mouth to say something more, but a rustling at the edge of the clearing draws his attention.

"Grey Morris?!"

He bites his tongue, stifling all the things he could say or scream. It's not their fault he's effective bait. He nods, buying a few more moments to compose himself.

"Wow. This is . . . such an honor." The young woman continues, and Grey smiles and thanks her for the compliments. He thinks Stefanie has vanished, but as he raises his flute to accompany the woman while she sings, he catches sight of her in the trees at the edge of the clearing, watching him with a sad smile.

AND ECHO

Lara Eckener

Speaker: Bodies are small and desire is large,
and we cannot always tell the difference,
between the body and desire,
between wanting to drink
down the whole of the world,
and only being capable of swallowing
enough to drown the creature kept
in our flooding and cavernous guts,
our overflowing spring mouths.
Bodies—too full to carry the echo
of the shout, too empty to not go
hoarse with hope and trying.

People: *What kind of a machine are we?*
We are small collections of immutable, drownable parts.

Speaker: Compasses who do not know a north,
bodies go spinning wild, searching for the sun,
without ever having seen the sun.
We search for light. We search for heat.
We find light. We find heat, but
there is no returning echo in response
to the way the sun means to keep us.
A body used to roaming does not know
how to make itself a home.

People: *What kind of an animal are we?*
A creature with every face, depending on the light.

Speaker: We are told stories about our faces,
their beauty and charm,
their fragility, sharpness, and hollows.
We may have even seen them once
as other people saw them,
but there was no responding echo.
No comforting voice. We don't know
what we're missing when we search
the mirror for the same face twice.

There is always a source of light
on the other side of the living liquid
tumble of quicksilver and glass,
fixed when we are fixed, moving
when we are moving, alive
and not, a soul and not.

People: *What kind of an ocean are we?*
We are thirsty and we fear that's the only thing about us that
might make us whole.

Speaker: We are sometimes overwhelmed by the sunsets,
the way the day does not wait for us
to understand her, the way she runs ahead,
dragging her heavy skirts across the sky
until we are trapped beneath them
in the intimate dark, the mystery of one less day left
for us to understand, the mystery
of how we did nothing but watch her go.

People: *What kind of a bird are we?*
We are brazen, dancing, chasing ourselves
the way we chase everything else.

Speaker: The truth of our bodies becomes a thing of myth,
this curiosity, this vanity larger
than any one creature could swallow.
We study our reflections in mirrors, rivers,
the faces of every person we meet.
It does not matter how large we become
in the eyes of others like us, there is no
responding echo. Every reflection rings hollow,
and we want so desperately to adopt
the faces given us.

People: *What kind of a tragedy are we?*
We will fall in love with a mask built by a stranger before we
will fall in love with ourselves.

Speaker: Bodies are small, but death is large.
A mountain valley every compass will lead to.
We come to it the way we come
to everything—waiting for the echo.
There is no echo, but there is mist, and wind,
and spare branches trembling under
the weight of the sky.
Death is so full there is not enough air
to carry that hopeful sound.

Death is so empty it's hard not to find
the reflection of ourselves in the river,
liquid tumble of quicksilver and glass
where we see cheeks
the shape of the warmth
we felt from the sun,
hair in a tumbling mane through which
we knew the shape of the wind,
empty mouth falling suddenly silent,
now that there is no yelling left to do.

People: *What kind of a revelation are we?*
We lean with the slow arc of time, come to fruition, press our
lips to the water.

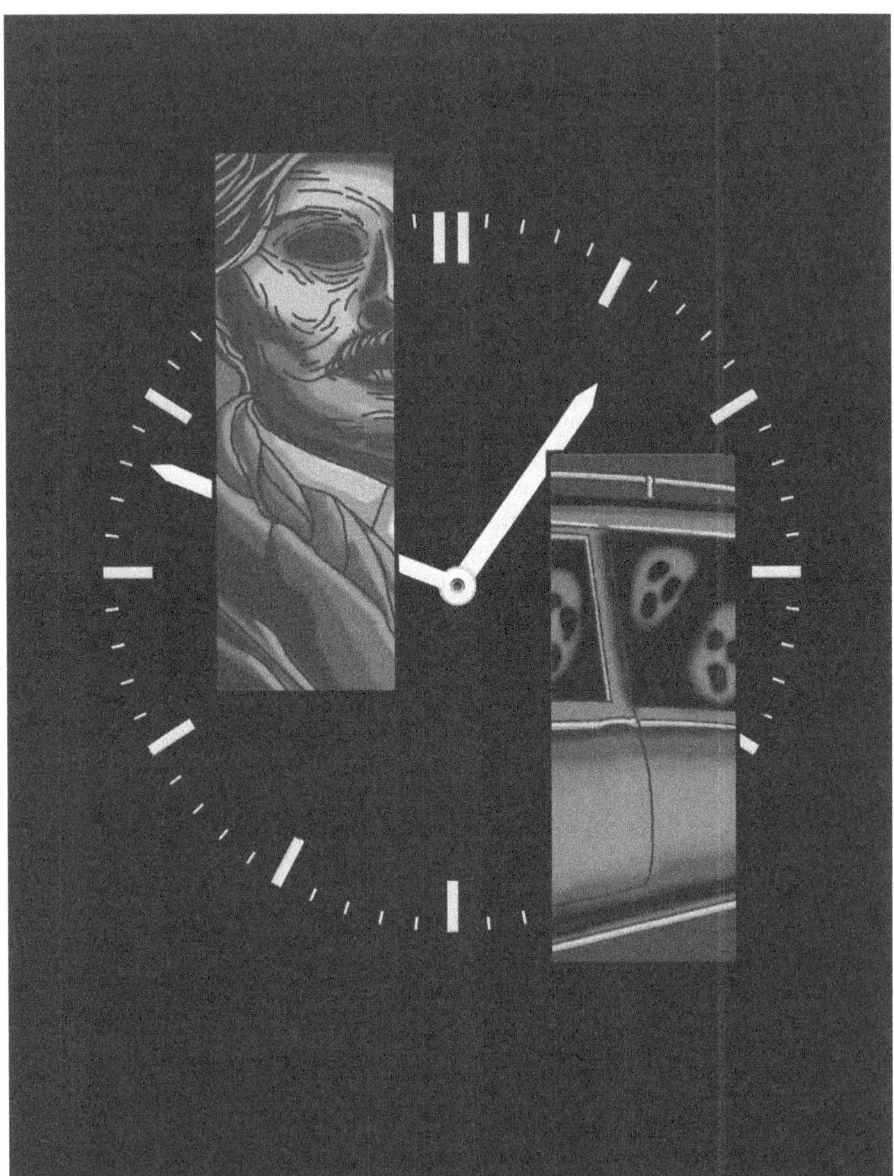

Tardy

Kaitlyn Sudol

Owen was constantly, chronically late.

"Terminally late," he would joke to people, grinning as they groaned at the pun.

He didn't *mean* to be late. It was always his intention to be on time for work, for gigs, for practice, for dates, for dinners out. As a child, when he was rushing out the door to get to school, sans breakfast and with only one sleeve of his jacket on, his mother would chide him.

"If you were going to hang out with your friends you wouldn't be late like this all the time!"

But that wasn't true. He was just as late with his friends as he was with less enjoyable obligations. It was just encoded into his DNA. The sun would rise, the tide would come in, the stars above would shine, and Owen would be late.

"You're very lucky that you've got that charming baby face," Javier has said to him more than once. "And you're even luckier that I'm easy for it. Not many other dudes would have waited forty-five minutes for their husband to show up to their own wedding."

Owen has long since given up offering excuses to those close to him—Javi, his mother, his sister Grace, his bandmates. They're used to it, for better or for worse, and not worrying about their reactions frees up enough mental real estate that worrying about the rest of the world's reactions isn't paralyzing the way it was when he was in college.

Because Owen can't help it. He truly, honestly, has worked hard his whole life to be on time, his efforts peaking his junior year of college when he more or less had a nervous breakdown over his own chronic tardiness. He tried setting alarms. He tried changing all the clocks in his dorm and car to run ten minutes fast. He tried telling his friends to lie to him about what time things started. He tried roping his parents into helping him by calling him before all of his classes and appointments to get his ass in gear.

None of it worked. Inevitably, he would sleep through his alarm or lose his phone or his car would need gas or he'd stop to help someone on the quad or he'd get all the way to the practice room and realize his violin was back in his dorm. By midterms that year, he'd stopped accepting invitations and even stopped going to some of his classes, tumbling full on into a depression that barely allowed him to get out of bed.

Javi was the one who eased him out of it. They were only friends, then, suitemates. He let himself into Owen's room and asked him what was wrong and sat there patiently as it all spilled out in nervous bursts of despair,

"I'm unreliable!" Owen had said at the end, pulling the blankets over his head to hide the tears that were on the cusp of falling. "I'm worthless!"

"Papi, your worth goes beyond your ability to show up where you're supposed to, when you're supposed to," Javi assured him, tugging the blankets down. "You're brilliant and talented and funny. People like you. In fact, people are more worried about you locking yourself away from the world than they ever were about you showing up places on time."

It wasn't exactly absolution, but between Javi's gentle tone and firm words, Owen began to accept that he was the way he was and the universe clearly just did not want him to be on time for anything, ever.

Years passed. College passed. Innumerable auditions passed. Countless shitty jobs passed. Being friends with Javi turned into dating Javi turned into marrying Javi. Teaching violin lessons turned into being a violin teacher at a hoity toity private school turned into . . . well. This.

He still can't quite believe the email in front of him. Whitman Music Academy is prestigious. It's well known. It's basically a seed school for half a dozen of the best university-level music performance programs in the country. And they want him to teach there.

Owen's been working hard, sure. And he's well known and well liked. Kids love him, he always gets on with the administration of schools he works at, and he has a real passion for helping kids find their own passion for music. Still, there's a reason he's teaching and not performing professionally—he's a good violinist, but he's not great. The music he writes is catchy, but the kind of catchy that translates into SoundCloud hits and minorly popular podcast theme songs, not the kind that translates into dollars.

"Maybe they sent it to me by mistake," he says abruptly, several hours later. He's in the middle of a mute dinner with Javi, still too stunned to put more than a few sentences together.

"I don't think they sent it to you by mistake," Javi assures him.

"I'm just not. . .that good," Owen says. "Like, objectively. I'm not that good.”

“Maybe you’re not the world’s best performer,” says Javi, who’s practically tone-deaf, “but you’re great with kids. You’re the one who says that teaching is more about reaching out to kids and helping them understand the material than mastering it yourself.”

“Yeah,” Owen says, “but that’s the sort of bullshit that someone who’s *not that good of a violinist* says to justify his employment the tenth time in a month he’s late for the morning staff meeting!”

“Someone was listening,” Javi says simply, which is a terrifying enough thought that Owen goes back to eating his dinner in wide-eyed silence.

After dinner, he responds to the request for an interview, then paces the living room in tight circles until Javi physically herds him down the hall and into bed.

It takes him a day to adjust to the idea that somewhere prestigious might want to employ him.

It takes him another day to get excited about the prospect.

It’s on the third day, the day before the interview, that dread sets in all over again.

Javi comes home to find him pacing the living room and tugging on his hair.

“Owen?” he asks slowly.

“I have to go to the interview,” Owen whispers.

“Ye-es?” Javi says. “That’s usually how the hiring process works?”

“I have to go to the interview!” Owen repeats. “Like . . . on time!”

It hit him mid-afternoon as he was working on a composition at the kitchen table. He’s going to need to make a good impression with these people. He’s going to need to seem professional and reliable. And he’s absolutely going to be late to the interview.

“Honey—” Javi starts to say.

“Don’t argue with me!” Owen snaps. “I’ve never been on time in my life! I only managed to swing my last job interview because it was literally a class on their campus that went over that caused me to be late. I’m going to be late to this interview and I’m going to sabotage my chances at getting this job!”

Three days ago, Owen didn’t even know if he wanted or deserved this job. Today, he’s already mourning the school year he was planning for in his head.

“Take it easy,” Javi says. “Come on, it’s not that hard to be on time. We’ll do it together—eat a nice dinner tonight, go to bed early, get a full night's sleep, get up early, have a nice breakfast here, and I'll drive you to the building so you don't have to worry about fighting with the buses, okay?"

Owen forces a smile that he doesn't feel. This is hardly the first time he's geared up with a foolproof plan for being on time, only to be late in the end.

"Not that hard," he echoes miserably, and prepares himself for the worst.

Dinner is fine. Getting into bed early was fine. Getting a full night's sleep. . .is not fine.

Owen spends the first three hours staring at the ceiling, catastrophizing—imagining, in great detail, an escalating series of mishaps, starting with oversleeping and ending with the whole house catching fire. He spends the next two hours trying to submerge himself in calming music and turn off his brain. At three am, he gives up and gets out of bed to take a walk around the house. Sometimes just getting out of bed is enough to remind him how much he would like to be IN bed, which in turn is enough to trick himself into getting sleepy.

The house is cloaked in the eerie silence of the witching hour. Javi and the cat are long asleep, and the floorboards seem thunderous when they creak under his feet. He circles the living room, eyes trained on the pools of moonlight on the floor as he pads across it.

He'll be fine. Everything will be fine. What's the worst that could happen? He flubs this interview entirely? He'll still have the job he has now. He'll still have his students and Javi and his home. At best, he gets something new. At worst, he loses nothing.

He'll be fine. Everything will be fine.

He's more or less tricked his brain into believing that, so he begins to creep quietly across the floor back to bed. Hopefully, the new mantra will last long enough to lull him back to sleep. He'll be a little tired tomorrow, but otherwise fine.

He turns towards the window, towards the glow of the moonlight, to take in a moment of the still summer evening, and then freezes.

There's a car in their driveway.

Not just a car, there's a hearse in their driveway.

Not just a hearse—he's not sure what it is. It's long and black. It's sinister. It looks like something out of his nightmares, and that's before he notices all of the pale, gaunt faces peering out the windows along the side of it. He takes an involuntary step back, so focused on the hearse that he misses entirely the man dressed in black standing at the bay window.

A scream lodges itself in Owen's throat, too shocked to break free.

The man at the window is wearing a suit from the turn of the century. His skin is nearly hanging off his face, sallow and waxy. His eyes are so dark that he doesn't seem to have a pupil at all, just deep, black eyes.

"We've room for one more," the man says.

It should be muffled by the glass, but Owen hears the words as if the man was standing in the living room with him. He stares at Owen through the glass and Owen stares back, motionless, until the central air kicks on. The sound of air blowing through the vents startles him out of his scared stupor and he nearly trips over himself in his rush to get back upstairs.

He's dreaming. He has to be dreaming. He stayed up too late freaking out over his interview and now he's having fucked up nightmares. That has to be the answer.

He stumbles back into the bedroom, panting hard despite the relatively short distance. He stops himself from slamming the door only at the last moment, but he still turns the lock and leans heavily against it, listening breathlessly.

No noise beyond the door, nothing aside from the central air.

It was a dream. It has to be a dream.

When he catches his breath, he sneaks across the room to the window. His hands shake as he parts the blinds and makes himself glance down at the driveway.

There's nothing there. The driveway is empty, apart from Javi's car.

"You're dreaming," he tells himself. "You're so nervous you're having a nightmare hallucination. Go to bed. Just. . .go to bed."

To his surprise, once he's back under the covers, he's asleep in seconds.

It's not that he forgets about the car and the man in the morning—quite the opposite. It's the first thing that pops into his mind when he opens his eyes. The second thing is that he's opening his eyes because the sun is in them, not because his alarm has gone off.

"Shit!" he shouts, and bolts straight out of bed, grabbing for his phone.

It's nine-thirty. Which is fine—it's fine, he tells himself, it's fine. He has plenty of time to get to his 10:30 interview. Just. . .an hour and a half less time than he allotted himself.

"Wake up!" he shouts at Javi, even as he barrels towards the bathroom. "We overslept!"

He turns on the shower and starts stripping, running back into the bedroom to grab a clean towel from a pile of laundry, just long enough to see Javi blinking sleepily at him.

"Oh fuck," he says once he squints at his alarm. "My alarm didn't go off."

"Mine either," Owen says, and then ducks back into the bathroom and all but jumps in the shower.

"We've got plenty of time!" Javi yells to him from the bedroom. "I'll go make you breakfast."

Owen takes a ten-minute shower and forces himself to take care as he dresses afterwards, grateful that he thought to lay out his interview outfit the night before. He gathers his messenger bag and his violin case and stomps down the stairs, only to find Javi waiting for him with a distinctly panicked look on his face.

Javi never panics.

"So, I have bad news, worse news, and better news," he says.

"Javi. . ." Owen says warningly.

"We lost power in the kitchen overnight," Javi says. "None of the appliances are working. And I just went out to get something from the car and I think maybe the battery is dead."

"Oh my god," Owen says.

"I"ve gotta say, honey, I knew, intellectually, that the universe has something against you ever being on time for anything, but this is. . . comically absurd."

"The *amount* that this is not helping right now—"

"Right, right," Javi says. "The better news is that at least there's time to call an Uber?"

They live half an hour outside of the city with no traffic. It's forty-five minutes until Owen's interview.

"Goddammit, fine!" Owen says to no one in particular, and pulls out his phone. He opens all his ride share apps, comparing prices and arrival estimates as quickly as possible.

Too quickly. The phone slips out of his hand and bounces on the floor. "*Shit!*"

He scoops it up quickly enough. The screen isn't cracked, thank god, but it flickers twice as he stares down at it. There's a new shared option listed. It's a cool ten dollars, at least a third of the regular price into the city, and the arrival is five minutes before his interview. He taps it automatically and the screen segues into the "locating driver" screen.

Then it flickers again. It keeps flickering as the driver's information pops up, the image of his face distorted by the strange ripples on his screen. It's not distorted enough to be unrecognizable, though, and Owen almost drops the phone again as the face of last night's man in black stares up at him.

He closes the whole program down as fast as his fingers will let him and chooses an option blindly from another app, sweating in his suit as the memory of his nightmare blooms again in the front of his mind.

"Honey, are you okay?" Javi asks. "You look. . .pale."

For a moment, Owen considers telling Javi about his nightmare. Then he sees the time and curses again.

"I'm fine," he assures Javi. "I'll tell you about it tonight. I've gotta run."

Javi grabs his wrist before he can make it to the door, though, and pulls him back for a quick, calming kiss.

"You're gonna do great," he says firmly. "You're going to get this job. It's going to be fine."

"I'm gonna do great," Owen repeats. "I'm gonna get this job. It's gonna be fine."

"Exactly," Javi says with a gentle smile. "Now go on. I'll see you later, okay?"

Owen kisses him one last time and then grabs his bag and violin case and races down to the end of the driveway to await his car.

Traffic is unbearable. Because of course it is.

Owen spends the entire drive staring at the clock on his phone, watching it move closer and closer to ten-thirty. He refuses to be late to this interview, but in his heart, he knows it's inevitable. This is just his life—late for every-thing, sabotaging himself around every turn without even trying.

The car gets stuck in bumper-to-bumper traffic four blocks from the building that houses the school's administration offices, which is Owen's cue to beg to be let out early and then sprint down the crowded, muggy sidewalks while fumbling to give his driver a disproportionately large tip out of guilt for jumping out early. He's a block away with six minutes to go, and blows through the building's doors with four minutes to go. It takes him a minute and a half to get the computers in the lobby to print out his visitor pass, and he knows he's a gross, sweaty, panicked mess by the time he skids over to the elevator bank, but as long as he gets on the next elevator, he will almost certainly be on time.

The elevator bank is packed. There are at least ten people standing around, maybe more. Owen tries not to pace as he watches the elevator numbers drop down and attempts to position himself nearest the one most likely to reach them first.

Luck isn't on his side—it is, of course, the one furthest away that dings and opens.

The rest of the crowd presses into the elevator, leaving just enough space for Owen to squeeze in with them if he holds his breath.

He steps towards the elevator, resigned to being gross and sweaty in close proximity to these people.

Then a hauntingly familiar voice says, "Room for one more."

Owen's head snaps up. Holding the elevator door open is the man in black. The man from last night. The man from his dream. The man from his ride share app.

He stands, frozen, in front of the elevator. He doesn't know how the others don't seem to notice how odd he looks, how terrifying. It's even worse in the harsh fluorescent lights that highlight just how inhuman his face is.

"I. . .I. . .um. . ." he stutters. "I'll. . .take the next one."

The man in black winks at him and pulls his arm back. The doors close and the elevator starts to climb. Owen stands, mutely staring at the closed doors, for so long he almost misses the next elevator that arrives in the lobby.

He's the only one left, now. He gets into the empty elevator and hits the button for the eighth floor. The doors close smoothly and it starts to rise, and things are just normal enough for Owen's previous concerns over his tardiness to creep in. He smooths down his suit and hair and tries to make himself look presentable in his reflection in the door.

It must have all just been a strange coincidence. His sleepy brain is linking together a series of events, projecting an image onto people who sort of look the same. That has to be it.

He passes the fifth floor and adjusts his tie.

That's when he hears the first creak.

It's distant. Muffled. It takes him a moment to figure out what it must be—something to do with the elevator mechanism, clearly.

Except there's music being piped straight into the elevators and it's pretty loud. If he's hearing this, it must be deafening in the shaft. He compulsively checks the inspection papers, but the car is fully up to date.

The creaking increases as he passes the sixth floor.

As he passes the seventh, there's a horrifying groan of twisting metal.

The doors open on the eighth floor just in time for a loud bang. He steps out and before the doors to his empty elevator close, the screaming starts.

Owen gets the job.

He's not surprised. It must have been hard to get other interviews in after the footage of twelve body bags coming out of the building played over and over on the evening news.

He doesn't see the man in black again.

He doesn't worry so much about being late, either.

PART II

Folklore

the traditional beliefs, customs, and stories of a community, passed through the generations by word of mouth.

The Hag's Hand

Nicole DeGennaro

Wander yonder far from home
The hag's hand'll get ya
Out too long once darkness comes
The hag's hand'll get ya
Awake at night, eyes open and bright
The hag's hand'll get ya

Something caught the hem of Ellie's skirt. It took her a moment of struggle to realize she was stuck, and then another to figure out the cause. She sighed and shifted the laundry basket to her other hip. But the cluster of weeds had already torn the fabric, adding one more thing to her mending pile.

She put the basket aside as she knelt down to free herself without causing further damage. As she worked, she hummed the tune of the rhyme that had kept her in line as a child. Now a wry smile accompanied it as she considered how silly it was that kids were threatened with *this*. A common weed that grew everywhere around the village and was notable only for being a nuisance.

But to a child, *hag's hand* sounded so ominous; it was easy for them to believe there was really a hag hiding beneath the dirt, waiting to catch disobedient children and drag them off into darkness. Never mind that in hindsight she could think of several terrible children who would have vanished quickly if the tales had been true. Up to a certain age, children couldn't reason away unfounded fear. It was only in that space that the hag lurked.

Now that she was older, she had adopted her Pa's opinion of the plant: a nuisance that often-marked infertile ground. Because the weed had never grown on her family's property, she hadn't thought about it or the rhyme in some time.

"

Ellie hissed as she pricked her finger on one of the nettles. She moved her hand away from her skirt, and the first drop of blood hit the dirt just short of the hem. The ground absorbed it and the subsequent drips almost faster than she could see, thirsty for any moisture in this dry season.

The wind shifted around her, carrying the scent of rain. But there wasn't a cloud in the sky.

As Ellie turned her attention back to the weed, she noticed the wheat-colored stalk of the hag's hand was turning dusty red at the base. As the color climbed toward the wispy frond still clutching her hem, her heart beat loud in her ears, drowning out the insect-like call of the grasshopper sparrows. When the color reached the nettles, the plant transformed before her eyes. A slender hand clutched her skirt where the frond had been, and as she watched it used one long needlepoint nail to trace looping red lines onto the pale fabric. The ink had to be her own blood, yet the message was using more than she had fed to the ground.

When it finished the last curl, she stared at the pattern in confusion. The hand withdrew, slithering away into the dirt. It all happened so quickly Ellie hadn't even thought to scream or try to flee. Instead, she followed the pattern with her eyes again. Luckily her Ma had taught her to read and write a bit despite Pa's indifference to her education. So on the second pass, she recognized that some of the loops spelled out her name in a strangely familiar cursive. It took her quite a bit longer to piece together the other word.

Beware, Ellie.

Her breath hitched as a cry clawed its way up her throat. She slapped a hand over her mouth and closed her eyes, fighting against the sense that the world had imperceptibly shifted around her. With her other hand she grasped the bloodstained fabric, debating whether to try and pull herself free from the nettles.

The wind shifted around her again. Her unsteady breaths filled her ears. Something gentle brushed across her cheek, too deliberate to be a strand of hair. It caught one of her tears and carried it away. *To hell with the skirt,* Ellie thought as she gave it a firm tug.

She met no resistance, so the force sent her tumbling backward. The breeze died. As she lay in the dirt trying to calm down, the relentless sun dried her tears until they were less than a memory. She feared what awaited her when she opened her eyes. But one minute passed, then another. A warm breeze came and went, leaving a lingering scent of sweetgrass. The buzzing song of the grasshopper sparrow slowly replaced the sound of her pounding heart. Its familiarity reassured her.

She opened her eyes. The clarity of the sky dazzled her—a bright, almost unnatural blue. Not a cloud in sight. The sparrow sang again and Ellie turned her head, catching a peek of its dusty brown feathers. The birds hid in the tall grass in an easy way she sometimes longed for, an effortless invisibility. Unable to learn that trick, she had taught herself how to spot them instead.

The bird noticed her and fluffed up before flitting away. She sat up. After one, two deep breaths, she looked at her skirt.

It was fine. No curling words, no bloodstains, no clinging nettles. In fact, there was no trace of the weed at all. She frowned, worried for a moment she had a sickness. Maybe the same one as her Ma. The one that had gotten so bad Pa had taken her to the doctor two towns over and had come back alone.

Then she saw it. The tear in her hem, exactly where the hag's hand had caught her. She ran her thumb over it for confirmation, then inspected her other fingers. A small drying dot of dark red on one tip marked her pinprick wound. Other than that, everything looked normal. But something unseen had changed. She felt it in her blood.

"Ya gotta tear in yer skirt," Thom stated as Ellie cleared the dishes from dinner. She didn't bother to spare Thom or the tear a look as she reached over for his plate. But a small tug in her stomach warned her to keep the details to herself.

"I tripped comin' home in the field," she said, remaining vague but accurate. Thom didn't reply straight away, but as was usual lately his stare dogged her. As if being the only woman in the household now made her suspicious.

"Well, take more care," he said. "There ain't money nor trade for more fabric thanks to the drought." She stifled a huff. It was his clothing she had to mend near every night; apparently, he couldn't put on his breeches without ripping holes in one or both knees.

"It's an easy enough fix."

"Ain't always gonna be."

The dishes clacked as she stacked them aggressively back on the shelf by way of reply.

"Thom," Pa said in a mild but warning tone. "Did you close up the coop for the night?" Since Ma had died, he'd been intervening more to counter Thom's increased scrutiny of Ellie. But never in a way where he actually scolded him for his behavior. After a long moment, Thom's chair scuffed against the stone floor. He went out into the yard without a word.

"Pay 'im no mind, Ellie." With Thom gone, she turned back to the room to face Pa. Firelight outlined his profile as he sat hunched at a small desk scribbling in the ledger. The descending curve of a frown had become a permanent fixture on his face. She waited for something more, some reason why she shouldn't mind, but he offered nothing.

With a frown to match Pa's, she grabbed the basin and went out to change the water. When she rounded the house, Thom stood near the coop, a solid mass of shadow leaning against the fence. The half-moon's dim light didn't reach his face, but her hair still stood on end the moment his gaze snared her.

A part of her wanted to freeze. Instead, she forced herself to turn away from him and continue to the pump. But as she dumped the grimy, days-old water and began to work the handle, her thoughts meandered back to Thom. He had changed so much in the few months since Ma's death. She knew they all had in some ways; a little of the light in each of their lives had dimmed.

But it affected Thom in a different way. Whereas she and Pa made an effort to focus on the remaining brightness, Thom allowed that sliver of darkness to encroach on what remained. All he could do was criticize and argue and sneer. His smile had become a phantom.

The pump handle interjected with a squeak as she continued filling the basin. But she hardly noticed. Thom wouldn't dare catch an attitude with Pa, so Ellie endured her brother's moods alone. She didn't know if Pa hadn't noticed the change in Thom or didn't find it concerning; either way, his response was to tell her not to mind, and to say nothing to Thom.

She started as something wet touched her foot; for a brief moment the hag's fingernail dripping with blood flashed in her mind. Then her wits caught up. She had overfilled the basin, and the water had spilled onto her. It had been irresponsible to let her attention wander since water was more precious than usual.

When she bent down to lift the basin, she caught a glimpse of herself in the dark surface. She froze. Her reflection was crying blood.

Her heart clamored as she reached up to wipe her face. Although her hand did not appear in the reflection, her fingers came away smeared in red. She gasped and then shot a glance over her shoulder to see if Thom had heard. He no longer lurked in the dark watching her, which was only a small relief.

Despite the lingering humidity, a chill crawled up her back and curled around her neck as she returned her attention to the basin. She prepared to plunge her hand into the water but paused as her fingertips skimmed the dark surface. There was no blood, or even a smudge of dirt that might have deceived her. After taking a deep, slow breath, Ellie gazed back into the water's abyss.

Blood still trailed down the reflection's face. But with her initial fright fading, she realized it wasn't her face at all. Where she expected soft brown eyes, full lips, and golden-brown skin all framed by straight black hair, instead a pale, wrinkled face with a bulbous nose and scraggly gray hair gazed up at her.

Or it would have been gazing at her, if it had eyes. Instead, two endless hollows sent her stomach tumbling, as if she had fallen into them and would fall forever. Despite the disorientation, she couldn't turn away. The hag wiped some of the blood onto one of her stubby fingers. Then she extended it toward Ellie.

It rose from the surface of the basin without disturbing the water. Everything in her periphery darkened until nothing existed but her and the hag. The finger paused when it touched her forehead, between and slightly above her eyebrows. She waited for it to continue through her skull or to gouge out her eyes or cause some other gruesome end.

Instead, gentle as a kiss, it traced a symbol onto Ellie's skin. Each sweep uncovered a strange ache within her; tears stung her eyes. When the hand withdrew into the basin, she almost reached in after it, her fears forgotten. But as soon as the fingertip receded below the waterline, the hag vanished.

Her tears fell then, creating waves in the confined ocean. In delicate lines of blood on her forehead, two semicircles faced one another, one smaller than the other and tucked inside the larger one. They hugged a star that sat between them.

The symbol stirred something in her, a specter of recognition. When she tried to chase it through her memories, it faded away so completely that she doubted its existence. In the end, the sigil meant nothing to her. But the tender gesture that had placed it on her skin reminded Ellie of her Ma, and that meant everything.

An owl hooted, bringing her back to her senses. The reflection in the basin was just her own, faint because the moonlight was so weak. She couldn't tell if the symbol was still on her forehead, but when she reached up to wipe it off, her hand came away clean. As she lifted the vessel and made her way back to the front of the house, she thought perhaps grief had changed her as much as it had Thom. Maybe he noticed the difference in her as she had noticed it in him, and that accounted for his recent watchfulness.

Something had certainly changed; even as a child she hadn't had a particularly active imagination. Now she was seeing things at random with no warning. The hallucinations were so real in the moment, but they made no sense. Afterward, she easily recognized the mix of childhood stories and fears, and adulthood rumors and warnings.

Out too long once darkness comes, the hag's hand'll get ya. . . she wanted to laugh at herself for getting so worked up over a childhood rhyme. But it only explained the content of the hallucinations, not why she was having them.

As she rounded the house with the basin in tow, a flickering sliver of light sliced through the darkness—the front door of the house had been left ajar. She began to push it open with her foot but paused at the sound of Pa's voice.

"Yer seein' things where they ain't," he said.

"Ya said the same 'bout Ma, and if ya'd listened to me things might'a ended different."

Pa paused for a long time before he answered.

"Bein' right once don't make ya right alw—"

Ellie pushed open the door, cutting off the conversation. They at least had the decency not to pretend they hadn't been talking about her; Thom looked right at her when she entered, and Pa still sat by the fire, updating the ledger. He probably hadn't even been looking at Thom while they talked.

"I'm back," she said, unnecessarily.

"'Bout time," Thom said. He snatched the basin from her hands, spilling some of the water onto the floor in the process.

She bristled. "It ain't a crime to enjoy the night air." She closed the door behind her, taking care not to slam it despite her annoyance. Thom would count any bad behavior as more evidence for whatever he thought was wrong with her.

"Some of us gotta git up early for the farm." He began to wash his hands and face in the basin as he prepared for bed. She glared at his back. Even though he was keeping a close eye on her, he still only saw what he wanted. Otherwise he wouldn't be so unaware of her own hard work. She made his meals, maintained his clothes, tidied his messes, shopped for his supplies, tended the fire. She did all that—and more, with Ma gone—and never complained.

Instead of continuing the argument, she took a deep breath and moved past Thom to gather the pile of mending from the bedroom. When she turned to exit, clothes bunched in her arms, he stood in the doorway. She moved toward him, expecting him to step out of her way, but instead he remained in place. Stifling a sigh, but unable to ignore the boiling of her blood, she met his eye.

"If yer wantin' clothes for yer farm work tomorrow, ya better let me by."

He smirked at her but moved aside. "Sure." He packed more scorn into it than a single word was meant to carry. She flowed past him and joined Pa by the fire without paying Thom any more attention. Pa glanced up and gave her a small smile; she received it like a treasure.

A field stretched as far as she could see in almost every direction. Ahead of her, beyond the long grass, stood the lone exception: a grove of trees that gradually filled out into a forest dark on the horizon. The aroma of sweetgrass and contentment hung in the air, and picturesque clouds waltzed across the sky.

She was dreaming, she knew. The edges of her vision had a blurry quality that even the beaming sunlight couldn't explain, and the peace permeating her had been lost to the past.

"Ellie!"

And this was the final clue, the most upsetting and welcome. Her Ma stood ahead of her, a little over halfway through the field. Closer to the forest than to her. She smiled and opened her arms to her daughter, her dark hair shimmering onyx in the light. Had the sun shone this bright since Ma had died?

She started toward her Ma with a grin. Her longing for one final hug had actual weight, a stone dragging her heart to the ground. When the grass parted around her, the scent shifted to that of damp, turned earth. But it wasn't raining, and each of her steps kicked up a small dust cloud. Even in this dreamscape the land wanted for water.

The wind seized her hair and tossed it in her face, obscuring her vision. She took a few more blind steps toward her Ma as she struggled to regain control of her hair. When she managed to clear it all and tuck it into her collar, she stopped short. Although most of the scenery remained the same as before, the hag now stood between Ellie and her Ma.

Daylight made her both more and less hideous. Dingy rags hung from her skeletal body, wafting in the wind. A shock of white, long hair fanned out around her, moving of its own accord. Her eyes appeared to be intact. With a thrill of fear Ellie understood this was a different hag than the one in the water basin. Among the soft gold grass and blinding blue sky, this hag stood as a gray blemish.

"Ellie, come along." It was her Ma's voice, but the hag's mouth had been moving. When Ellie peered past her, she saw Ma motioning her forward.

Beware, Ellie. Was this what the warning had been about?

The hag lifted a twisted hand, the swollen joints forcing it into that permanent position. Unable to articulate the fingers, she pointed the entire claw at Ellie. Then she opened her arms wide, as if mocking Ma's welcoming gesture. Tears stung Ellie's eyes. If she wanted to reach her Ma, she would have to pass the hag.

She attempted to go around her, moving left slowly at first and then working up to a run. Her lungs burned as she pushed herself to increase the distance. But when she turned back toward the center of the field, planning to race to her Ma, the hag still faced her, blocking the way. No matter her speed in any direction, the hag moved with her. There would be no avoiding her.

"Ma," she called; it sounded more like a frightened cry than she liked. "I dunno what to do! What should I do?"

For the first time, Ellie wondered if the hag had killed her Ma or driven her insane. Up until her own encounter, she had always thought it a fable. But what if it were all real, and after dispensing with Ma the hag had now targeted Ellie? Ma might be trying to warn her, or protect her.

Her Ma started to answer, but then the hag spoke over her.

"What do the dead know of what the living should do?" the hag asked.

Ellie ignored her and tried to peer around at her Ma again.

"Ma. Please!"

In a flash, the hag stood mere steps from Ellie, casting a long shadow over her.

"Following her path shall lead you to the same end, child."

Ellie woke, with tears on her face, in the dark.

At first, she wouldn't admit it to herself.

When she went to run errands in town, she'd cut along the edges of her neighbors' properties instead of following the road. She'd meander while doing laundry, or go looking for wild flowers to put in the house. She gazed into pools of standing water, or tried to spot weird movements in the corner of her eye.

She wasn't the only one in denial, either. Despite her coming home with boots caked in mud or burrs hugging her skirt, Thom said nothing. He would pass her in town or out in the fields with nothing more than a casual glance. He kept their evening talk to pleasantries. She didn't know if Pa had given him a scolding after all, but either way she was grateful her interactions with Thom were going well. Because her search for the hag was not.

After a fruitless week, and her frustration mounting, she stopped trying to fool herself. But only because she had to accept that she couldn't find more hag's hand. The rhyme said nothing about how to locate it, because it was meant to be avoided. So instead she followed the song as if it were instructions, but even that failed. The hag's hand wouldn't be tricked. It only appeared when it wanted, and until then she would have to wait.

She didn't have a full understanding of why she wanted to find the hag again—just thinking about her eyeless face and husk of a voice froze the breath in her lungs. But it also sent a strange thrill through her veins.

Each dreamless night that passed, she thought more about the hag and her Ma. They had all become linked in her mind, a tether tying the three of them together somehow. In the dream she had feared the hag had killed Ma and now moved down the line to Ellie. In daylight, the fear crumpled, the shape of it too simple. But she couldn't discern its true form. And if her Ma couldn't help her understand, maybe the hag could.

That alone might not have been enough to propel her search. There was also the matter of the thing inside her. Something had shaken loose after her encounter with the hag's hand. Now it rattled around demanding attention, becoming more insistent as time passed. But that, too, she couldn't identify and thus could not fix. Was it something weighing her down? Did it have to be returned to its proper place, or expelled?

Perhaps there was no sense to be made. But her mind kept worrying at it, certain it was a puzzle that needed solving. So she sought the hag out of fear and curiosity. Out of desire and necessity.

Another week passed. The fields grew gaping dirt mouths pleading for water as the drought continued. The clear blue sky taunted flora and fauna alike; the bright sun cooked everything alive. Thom ended up at home more and more as the crops died in the fields, and the reprieve from his scrutiny ended as he grew restless. Worry aged Pa years by the day.

"Where ya goin' every day?" Thom asked, cornering her by the door one sweltering morning. She blinked up at him, then glanced down at the laundry basket wedged between her arm and hip. It only held a few items, but Ellie had been doing laundry every day now for a week. It gave her an easy reason to go outside, and the fact that the river had become more mud than water provided an excuse for her wanderings.

Thom followed her gaze and frowned.

"Don't seem like clothes need washin' each day," Thom said, stating it as an observation to the empty house. He met her eyes again. "The rest of yer chores ain't gittin' done."

The loose thing within her had been distracting her all morning, becoming so loud she could hardly focus. She hoped it meant she would find the hag today. If she could get out the damned door.

She tried to shove past her brother. But Thom stood firm, a strange glint in his eye although he said nothing more. The combination of the heat and his attitude sparked the tinder of her impatience.

"Yer welcome to sweep or tidy if ya want, since ya ain't doin' nothin' else." The strength of her voice surprised her, and her posture straightened to match. She stood firm under his skeptical gaze. The way Thom's eyes widened for a moment revealed his own shock. But it quickly gave way to a blank expression she suspected masked something worse.

She pressed the laundry basket to his chest. "Or why don't ya go do the washin'? I'd rather stay outta the heat." He didn't move to take the basket, so she gave it another push against his chest. A strange snarl curled his lip for a second before his face became a mask once more. After a few tense moments, Thom stepped aside.

Ellie replaced the basket between her arm and hip and pushed the door open. As she stepped into the sunlight, Thom spoke.

"Good thing Pa ain't here to see ya right now."

She stopped, expecting the words to wound her as Thom intended. Instead she absorbed them, and they transformed in the alchemical fire of her heart. Then, without turning around, she opened her mouth and spat them back at her brother.

"Y've disappointed him more'n I ever could."

Thom rushed toward her, a brief scuff the only warning of his rapid approach. Before he could lay a hand on her, she kicked the door shut in his face. Then she strolled out into the field as if it were any other morning. She expected him to burst out of the house in pursuit. But after a few minutes of walking in silence she paused glanced back. The door remained closed. She allowed herself a satisfied smirk as she continued on her way.

Her heart was still thundering in her chest when she reached the river. With her impatience and anger fading, she found the fear that had been lurking underneath. Her legs wobbled, and she sank to her knees by the muddy water. Thom had been right. Pa would've been horrified by her behavior.

But her shame was momentary, slipping away from her like a minnow, flashing in the sun and then gone from sight. Instead, laughter bubbled out of her, and she covered her mouth to try and stifle the sound. Telling her brother off shouldn't have made her so giddy. It had been a unique pleasure, though, after months of biting her tongue. Thom might tell Pa about it, and she might be punished, but any consequences were too distant for concern. With the sun warming her skin and the breeze tousling her hair, she was triumphant and free. No cage could contain her; no blow could bring her down.

She set the laundry basket aside, the water being too shallow and murky for clothes washing. Instead, she slipped off her shoes, hiked up her dress, and waded in. The lukewarm water didn't provide much relief, but the mud between her toes brought its own kind of comfort. Maybe she could root deep, plant herself here to grow tall and unstoppable as any tree. When she peered at her feet, she caught sight of her jubilant reflection. On her forehead, the strange symbol had reappeared, glowing warm and bright. And the loose thing within her had quieted.

She didn't find the hag that day, but she hardly noticed.

When she got home in the late afternoon, Thom was gone. He hadn't done any chores.

The silence that followed him home for dinner chilled the air, but a protective shroud surrounded Ellie, as if she had fished it out of the river. Her impenetrable calm agitated Thom; although he said nothing, he shot cold knives at her with his glances, trying to find a weakness in her barrier. She met each one with a gentle smile. Pa chattered about the drought and the goings-on around town, either oblivious to or uncomfortable with the hostile quiet.

That night, she saw her Ma again. She came in a dream disguised as a memory, or maybe a memory disguised as a dream. Ellie knew some parts were recollections but couldn't distinguish the real from the imaginary.

Ma stood with her at the edge of their family's field in the waning sunlight. Pa called to them, expecting dinner soon. Ellie moved to return home, but Ma wrapped an arm around her shoulders, turning her back to the horizon. She hugged Ellie close to her side, and for a few quiet moments they watched the stars wake in the sky.

With the hag nowhere in sight, she held her Ma close. The faint scent of sage from old lady Mabel's homemade soap greeted her; it had been the one small indulgence Ma had allowed herself. Ellie never expected to smell it again, not being allowed any indulgences of her own. It helped mask the acrid sulfur odor of the river water that clung to all their clothes.

"There's so much more than this," Ma whispered. Her eyes remained on the horizon, her voice even more distant. When her heartbeat increased just so, Ellie's stuttered to match. Their pulses mingled where Ma's bare wrist rested against her daughter's neck. Now that Ellie knew loss and longing, she recognized that distance in Ma's voice: the gap between dream and reality.

Ma's heart had been weighed down too, and Ellie had never known. "And there's nothin'—" Ma stopped and cast a quick glance over her shoulder, the corners of her mouth turned down slightly and her eyes alight with anxiety. Deeming it safe, she turned back to the horizon, flat as anything but still piled with promise.

"There's nothin' in the stars says it can't be ours."

As she said the word *stars*, a group of them sparked to life, as if she had spoken them into existence. Ellie craned her neck but saw nothing written there.

It was a lesson she wasn't yet prepared to learn.

Ma gazed upward and closed her eyes. She breathed deep and smiled as she exhaled, her golden brown skin shining in the starlight. As she raised up on the balls of her feet, almost like she might float toward the heavens, Pa called to them again. The ethereal sheen drained from Ma in an instant, as if his voice had tethered her to the ground.

In a rapid motion she turned to Ellie and crouched down to her level. But now her face was the hag's face, with sightless voids instead of eyes. For a moment Ellie thought she saw stars twinkling in them too. She reached up and cupped Ma's cheek, who leaned into the touch with a smile.

"Ya have to help her," Ma whispered. But now her voice came from behind Ellie as the woman in front of her became more like the hag by the second. She dropped her hand and spun around. Ma was addressing the hag, and Ellie stood unacknowledged between them as the hag rose to her full height.

"Nay," the hag said, unmoved by the pleading note in Ma's voice. Her head tilted down, as if she sensed Ellie's presence. "She has to help herself."

"Witch!" Thom's voice sliced through the darkness, much closer than Pa's had been.

The hag receded into the shadow until she vanished, and Ma stepped in front of Ellie just as a group of villagers appeared around them. Most of their faces were obscured, but Thom stood front and center holding a blazing torch.

"Ya witch, y've doomed our whole family," Thom hissed. A hellish fury contorted his face, and Ellie cowered. Ma stood firm, staring him down. Then she raised her arms, and all the lights—the torch, the stars, the moon—were extinguished.

Something gentle brushed against her face, a feather or a wisp of hair, and then the dream darkness settled more heavily around her. It took her a few moments to realize she had woken up. Her heart beat so fast it was almost one continuous contraction, and her breaths were only small gasps.

Everything whispered danger to her, from all directions. But as her eyes adjusted to the dark, with help from the coals of the banked fire, no threats appeared. It must have been a lingering feeling from the dream.

She rolled on her side, her heart relaxing and her breath slowing. But she was too worked up to fall back asleep. She remembered that conversation with Ma, and she still didn't quite understand it. Except now she recognized the pattern in the stars: the sigil that had been traced on her forehead. But did that part belong to reality or imagination?

Either way, the dream had opened a new ache in her, because it revealed what she missed most about Ma. Everything was harder now, but she longed for those private moments and that secret knowledge. It might not have made sense to her at the time, but she knew the shape of a key, and she knew to keep it close.

But she only had the one, and there must be more. Perhaps what had been rattling around inside her was not something loose, but something locked. And the only key she had didn't seem to fit.

Without Ma, she had no help. It was knowledge Pa and Thom didn't possess and thus could not impart. Something that if they knew, they might fear, because they couldn't fathom it or its importance to her. They treated her like glass, but they were the fragile ones, choosing to be afraid because it took less effort than trying to understand.

Beware. Take a different path. Help yourself.

There, in the dark, Ellie pieced together the other key, the one the hags had given her. And this one unleashed what the lock had been restraining.

When she felt a familiar tug at the hem of her skirt, she tried not to get her hopes up. But she still ensured no one had followed her before glancing down.

The start of a jubilant laugh slipped from her when she recognized the frond of the hag's hand grasping her skirt. But she suppressed the rest of it, still haunted by Thom's contorted face from her dream.

Luckily, she wasn't far from the stream that had once been the river, and her brother never bothered to come out this far. Nobody really did anymore, except Ellie. So she knew this cluster of hag's hand hadn't been in the area yesterday, or the day before, or the whole two weeks she had been searching. Yet now the remaining loose fronds bent in the breeze, beckoning to her. She reached out and ran her finger against the wisps, following the curve of the nettles so they were silk against her skin instead of spines. The gentle touch eased a tight coil of anxiety that had wrapped around her heart.

With a smile, Ellie knelt down and placed the nearly empty laundry basket aside. She spread her skirt around her and set to work extricating the nettles, managing it without accidentally pricking a finger. After reassuring herself that the only witnesses would be the grasshopper sparrows, she pierced her finger with one of the fine, sharp points on the weed. She hissed despite expecting the pain. The sound shifted as it slithered out of her, becoming a strange buzz and then rising until it blocked out all other noise, until it shook her bones.

Blood welled on her fingertip and then splattered onto the ground: one, two, three drops that the dirt eagerly drank. The cacophonous sound ceased, so sudden and absolute it knocked the wind out of her like a blow. Whorls of dust danced on the breeze; the ground continued to lap up her blood as she let it fall. The stalk of the hag's hand shifted colors again, from beige to a purplish red. It raced up toward the fronds, and in an instant Ellie was staring at a wiry arm with long fingers and pointed nails instead of a weed. She waited for it to write her another message.

Instead, the hand braced itself against the dirt. A second arm had appeared in the cluster and mimicked the motion. The ground quaked. She backed away, fumbling for the laundry basket as it upended. The arms tensed with effort, thin muscle straining under the dusty skin. A mound emerged at the base of the weeds, raising up until it stood almost a head taller than her. Soil cascaded from the form until it revealed the hag that had been buried beneath. She crouched before Ellie, almost bent double as her shoulders heaved from the effort of emerging. She remained that way for a few moments, and then she lifted her head to meet Ellie's eyes.

She had expected the eyeless hag or the one with the clawed hand. Instead, this was yet a third hag. She had an unwavering stare, like a wolf about to leap at the throat. But the eyes themselves were the most unnerving. One was a black so complete and endless it appeared to be an empty socket until it caught the light. The other was an opalescent white, its surface a swirl of shifting colors. The hag's mouth cracked into a crooked smirk. A mixture of blood and saliva oozed between her lips, sliding down her chin and dripping onto the ground in long strings.

In shock, Ellie lost her grasp on all the questions she had hoped to ask; they flitted away like birds, hiding in the tall grass. The hag, undisturbed by the silence, settled herself onto the ground across from Ellie with an almost relieved sigh. Then she closed her eyes and tilted her head toward the sun. The smirk melted into a soft smile.

This revealed that most of the hag's teeth had been destroyed. Where they weren't missing entirely they remained as jagged fragments that had reduced her gums to a mush of continually bleeding wounds.

"Time's slipping, child," the hag gurgled as she reluctantly turned away from the sun's warmth and toward Ellie. "Why've you summoned me?" Blood-flecked spittle flew from her mouth when she spoke.

But the word *summoned* worked a kind of magic in Ellie—not all of it welcome. While it sent a thrill through her, it also conjured the image of Thom screaming *Witch!* A pit of dread opened in her stomach. Of course this was witchcraft, and she had been participating in it while denying it to herself. The hags had given her a key to unleash something within her, but she had chosen to use it. Perhaps it had released something that should have stayed constrained.

Yearning had warped her perspective, and she had rationalized her behavior instead of facing reality. Ma was not trying to reach her through the hags. And she wasn't an innocent target of their trickery, either. In fact, something about the hags had always felt familiar, and she had never wrestled with a true fear of them.

The thought of Ma brought tears to her eyes. Her hope that there might be some magic that could reunite them slipped away. Ellie had to let her go.

"Ya...yer not my Ma." It wasn't a question, exactly, but she felt the need to say it all the same.

For a moment the swirling colors of the hag's white eye paused, as if reacting to the grief in Ellie's voice. "Nay, your mother is dead. You saw her buried yourself."

That was half true. Ellie had seen the casket lowered into the ground, but a part of her had hoped Ma hadn't been inside. She began to sob there in the field before the hag, the first time she had cried for her loss since the funeral. The void that her Ma's death had opened within her carried more weight than she thought she could bear.

The hag did not interrupt Ellie's tears, and eventually they ceased. But they had not drowned her curiosity.

"Was Ma a witch? Am I?" She figured it was worth having her suspicions confirmed. As she waited for the hag's answer, she expected her dread to consume her. After all, being a witch would be a death sentence. Yet a strange sort of comfort unfurled inside her instead: the peace of seeing things for what they were.

The hag watched her for some time in silence, as if her uncanny eyes allowed her to see Ellie's internal transformation. Then she leaned forward until their noses almost touched. Only the dark right eye showed a reflection. The left one remained a shifting, shimmering white.

"Do you know what a witch is, girl?"

She thought it was rhetorical, so she didn't answer until the hag let the question linger.

"A woman what speaks to the Devil." Ellie frowned. The preacher could spin whole sermons on the evils of witchcraft, yet it all came down to that simple description. But as she spoke the words herself, they rang false.

"Tastes sour, eh?" The hag chuckled. "A man shan't speak a woman's truth. Aye, you're a witch. Every woman is a witch when need calls." She tilted her head so only her black eye watched Ellie, the white one hidden by the slant of her nose. "But most times she's just a woman." The chuckle became a full laugh, a sound like rain beating a rooftop. "Just!" She almost couldn't catch her breath from the force of her laughter.

Ellie wasn't sure she understood. But she knew the shape of a key.

"And what's a hag?" she asked. The hag's laughter dissipated, quick as a summer storm. She nodded, as if pleased, and then turned her gaze back toward the sun. All the humor had drained from her face.

"A woman what survived being a witch."

The note of longing in her voice snagged Ellie as surely as the nettles, and she wondered if that yearning lived in every woman. The rustling grass and distant sparrow calls filled the quiet that settled between her and the hag. She had no sense of how much time, if any, had passed. It seemed arbitrary.

The hag's attention snapped back to her, and she gasped in surprise.

"Will you embrace or shun your magic, child?" Her steady gaze shifted past Ellie in alarm, as if she had heard something. Then she vanished.

Ellie hadn't blinked, hadn't looked away. Yet now instead of staring down a hag, she watched as a sparrow hopped out of the grass and pecked at the empty ground in front of her. She sat in a small clearing where the hag's hand had once been, her only companion the overturned laundry basket.

Yet she didn't feel alone at all.

The world had darkened, although it was well before sunset. Ellie glanced up. At some point a flock of clouds had cluttered the sky. But not just any clouds; these were deep gray, ripe with rain. It had been so long since clouds had obscured the sun that she had forgotten how it changed the light.

The wind hadn't kicked up yet, so she knew she had some time before the rain would fall. Still, she quickened her pace. The hag's words trailed her like a cat, sometimes slinking just out of sight and other times swiping at her until she couldn't ignore them.

She didn't yet know if she wanted to embrace her magic. What kind of need could it fulfill? It seemed to her that women who used it met terrible ends. And she doubted the hag's assertion that all women were witches. Because if it were true, there would hardly be any mothers, sisters, or daughters left alive. So most of them had to be just women.

Without warning, the clouds ruptured, pelting the ground and Ellie and everything with fat droplets of water. She scooted under the roof awning and edged around the house to the front door. The rain came faster than even the thirsty earth could imbibe it, and it turned to mud beneath her feet. As the rain struck the roof, the hag's laughter echoed in her head. *Just!*

She nudged the front door open with her shoulder. "Pa, it's rainin'!" she called, even with the noise of it bouncing around their small house. He smiled at her from his chair by the fire.

"It's a welcome blessin'," he said. The clouds had gathered so thick it had turned almost midnight dark outside. The firelight cast long shadows around the room. Ellie closed the door and moved toward Pa, laying her damp skirt on the hearth to dry.

When she turned around, a hollow-eyed specter stood in the doorway to the bedroom. A small yelp escaped her before she realized it was Thom. The knowledge only deepened her fear. He stepped toward her, and when she caught sight of his eyes, she preferred the hollows the darkness had painted. The firelight danced in his gaze, just like the torchlight had in her dream.

Everything whispered danger.

"What's there on yer skirt?" Thom asked, his voice strange and hoarse. She glanced down, the spots of red almost glowing at the hem. Her finger had continued to bleed while she had spoken with the hag, and Ellie hadn't paid it any mind.

"It's blood, Thom," she said, hoping the slow and deliberate use of his name might call him back to himself. Because this person was not her brother. "I nicked myself on the fence."

But he didn't hear her. At the word *blood* he shot forward, closing the distance between them before she could react. He wrapped a hand around her throat; she had never noticed how big his hands were, how slender her own neck.

"I *knew* it," Thom hissed as he lifted her up, just enough that she couldn't keep her footing. "Yer just like Ma. I *told ya.*" The last part he directed at Pa. "Out in the field with yer blood magic, cursin' the crops, makin' us all starve." He squeezed her throat and Ellie gasped. Tears stung her eyes as bursts of light flashed in her vision. She tried to slip her fingers between Thom's hand and her throat, tried to peel his fingers back, tried to claw his face, his arm. He smirked the more she struggled.

"Thom!" Pa yelled, and then he was there trying to separate them. But Thom's crazed righteousness granted him a strength even Pa couldn't match, and Ellie's nails were too short to break his skin.

Until they weren't. Before her eyes, her hand became the hag's, with slender fingers and long, pointed nails. She wasted no time sinking them into the soft skin of Thom's forearm.

"Ya feckin' witch," he growled in pain as beads of blood rose on his arm. He didn't let her go, but his grip loosened enough that she sucked in some air and got her feet back on the ground. Then she kicked her brother in the groin.

He doubled over with a wheeze, releasing Ellie. Pa immediately took a place between them. "Yer the only one actin' possessed here, Thom. What's gotten into ya?"

A fear rang in Pa's voice that she had never heard before. Thom stumbled toward the door, and she didn't want to wait for what he would do next. She glanced at her hand, which was her own again. Remembering her dream, she closed her eyes as Ma had done, and then she raised her arms.

The fire went out, pitching the room into darkness.

"I'll see ya on the pyre with 'er, then," Thom spat. She had crept away until her back hit the wall, hoping to stay out of his grasp. But there was no need for the retreat. He opened the door and fled into the rain.

"Witch!" he screamed into the storm, his voice as terrible as it had been in her dream. "Git the irons; Ellie's a witch!"

She heard her Pa fumbling around in the dark, but she had no problem navigating, everything coming into clear focus as if the fire still burned. She headed for the door.

"Ellie?" Pa whispered. She froze. Instead of anger or terror, she heard that sad longing that had become so familiar to her as of late. He managed to light the lantern on the table, turning it down low, just enough that they could see one another in the darkness.

He knelt before her as more voices began shouting through the storm. He cast a fearful glance toward the door before turning back to his daughter.

"Ya gotta run," he said, the words so low and quick it took her a few seconds to decipher them. "I won't let 'im take ya like he took Ma."

He pulled her into a hug as the shouts approached the house, holding her so close his thudding heart banged against her ribs. Then he let her go. "I love ya."

She ran into the rain. It cascaded around her, more curtain than water. She pushed her way through, ducking behind the house and across the field. The steady pounding of the downpour masked the thud of her footfalls, and instead of slipping in the mud, she found every sturdy place to step without looking. And the ground swallowed her footprints behind her.

But when she risked a glance back, covered lanterns bobbed in the darkness as people gave chase, some close enough that she could make out silhouettes. Shadows coming to swallow her whole.

She didn't think; she just ran. At first, she had no destination, but then almost before the image came to her mind, she adjusted her course for the forest. It was further away in reality than it had been in the dream when Ma had beckoned her toward the woods. Now, Ellie would obey. She hiked up her skirt as the drenched fabric threatened to trip her.

Lightning arced across the sky ahead, as if pointing the way, showing she had covered more ground than she had thought. Maybe she wouldn't be safe in the woods, but it would afford her more places to hide. Her lungs strained and her throat burned where Thom had crushed it. But she wouldn't stop. She would make it. She would survive being a witch.

"Yer gonna burn, Ellie!" Thom shouted behind her, closer than she would have liked. But the trees rose up to meet her, the gnarled oaks and looming pines. With just a few yards to go, a hand clawed at her back, trying to find purchase on her blouse. But the waterlogged fabric hugged her skin, and before Thom could try again, Ellie crossed into the forest.

Protective arms reached out of the darkness and enveloped her, one resting gently, so gently, against her mouth. Another wrapped around her waist and pulled her close, then backed her further between the dense trees. Thom burst into the woods only seconds later and skidded to a halt. The arms holding her froze, not wanting to risk drawing his attention. She recognized the knobby joints on the hand resting over her mouth, and her knees went weak with relief. She had made it to the hags.

But Thom continued the hunt. He carried no lantern, so he crouched to try and find footprints among the needles and leaves. He sought broken branches, scraps of fabric, any hint of where she had gone. But there were no signs. The forest belonged to the hags, and it would hide her in its shadows.

To her brother, it would look like she had vanished. More proof his sister was a witch.

No one followed Thom into the woods. Either they had lost the trail or were too afraid. Her brother refused to give up for quite some time, pulling small branches off trees in frustration, snatching at nothing as if he might pull her from the air. Eventually, with a frustrated scream, Thom abandoned the hunt.

"If ya ever show yer face again, I'll kill ya!" he yelled, facing the wrong direction. His words died on the air, and from the way he shuddered she knew it unsettled him that the trees wouldn't carry his message like they should.

He left, with one last look into the darkness. The rain stopped. After waiting a few more moments, the hands unfurled and Ellie stepped away. Then she turned.

Among the trees stood the hags, although they looked more like women now. She spotted the one with the deformed hands, whose fingers had been broken so she couldn't write the runes. The one with the broken teeth, which had been shattered so she couldn't speak the spells. And the one whose eyes had been gouged out so she couldn't lay the curse.

Or had the runes been misshapen letters from struggling to write? Had the spells been normal words twisted by a speech impediment, and the evil eye just a squint to compensate for failing vision? As she saw the human side of the hags, she couldn't be sure of the truth. But the last key they had given her slipped into its rightful lock, and she understood how a woman was never just a woman.

A laugh floated out of her, and she let it loose, reveling in the way the trees bounced it back to her until it became a chorus. As she moved toward the three women who had helped save her, more emerged from the shadows. Some were much older than her, some perhaps younger. Some weren't women at all, but others who had been forced to find their magic to survive.

There were dozens, almost as many as the trees, as if the forest expanded each time it saved a life. And, like her, they each had the same glowing sigil on their forehead. She had joined a glorious coven.

They opened their arms to Ellie, and she ran smiling into their embrace.

You May Yet Find Them Blind

Lara Eckener

You may yet find them blind—

Breath, the movement in the branches,
skin pressed into ash white bark,
color of waiting, bleached of shadow,
spirits standing in the sun feel nothing,

we become our own suns, always
resisting the urge to burn all away,
ghosts sown across highway shoulders
grow in our wake, each mile
over restless bones, a rap against a door
men imagine they have the authority to close.

You may yet find them disquiet—

Godhood, girlhood,
yearning for the world that is not ours,
though it should be,
though we could pull it apart,

wind will blow through trees
as breath through stifled throat,
from light grows the absence of light
there are souls caught in the branches
there are bones, there is a memory
of what it means to be alive.

You may yet find them burning.

ACROSS THE RIVER

Kaitlyn Sudol

February 28

It is our first night in our new home, and it seems fitting that this should be the first night I write in a new journal.

Father has thrown away my last journal, just like the one before it. "If you spent less time whining in that book, you'd have more time to take care of the baby!" he said as he threw it away.

Assuming it would be hidden under my bed was an error now, I know. And I should probably stop writing altogether—he's probably right. But our new home is in the middle of nowhere, miles from town, and we're hours from the few friends I had at our old home in Riverville. I fear that if I don't have some kind of outlet for my thoughts, I will never be able to survive.

But while this house is new to us, it is very, very old, and full of many hidden nooks and crannies. There is a small piece of molding down by my dresses that can be pulled away from the wall, and that's where this journal will stay. It's somewhere he would never think to look, and it means that my thoughts can be mine again.

Toby starts school in two days' time. Father has decided that there's no further need for me to attend school, that I should focus on keeping the house and watching the baby. I don't know how I'll meet anyone if I'm in this house all day.

I miss my mother. It's been six months now, since her disappearance. Toby and I both balked at the idea of leaving Riverville while she was still missing. What if she comes back, looking for us? How will she find us? But Father was adamant that we leave before the thaw. ~~He claims he left to find a better job, but I fear he knows more about her disappearance than he lets on.~~

Anna has begun to cry. I need to tend to her before he hollers at me for it.

March 2

It has only been two days, but I fear my prediction has been correct so far. I leave the house only to do the laundry in the river. Father keeps complaining that I should be preparing to marry, but I don't see how I'm to meet anyone if I'm in the house all day. If I even wanted to meet a boy. Which I don't. Besides, who would care for the baby and prepare meals and do the cleaning around the house if I were to leave? Not Father, surely, and with Toby in school, there is no one else.

I'm not sure if that's a good thing or a bad thing. It will keep me from being married off too quickly, yes, but I don't relish being here, either.

March 6

Anna hasn't stopped crying for two days. I walk with her outside to keep her from enraging Father further. He threw a pot at me yesterday, as if her wailing is my fault. I'm afraid that he may try to hurt her, next.

March 7

It is very late.

I worry, to be honest, that we are all alone out here. Miles from town. No neighbors within sight. The isolation is frightening, especially when Father is in one of his tempers, and especially at night.

Especially on nights when I swear I can hear someone speaking to the baby in the room next door.

Father has been asleep for hours. I can see Toby curled up in the bed across from me. And yet, the whispering continues.

Anna has calmed in the past two days, but the whispering persists. I know I should go out and check on her, but I am afraid.

March 9

I have asked Father to allow us to switch bedrooms. I was afraid that he would react badly, but after another night of hearing someone talking to the baby, I knew I had to do it. I waited until he was done with dinner, full and content, and made sure to insist we would move all the furniture ourselves and stress that this would make it easier for me to take care of the baby. I was surprised that he agreed, but it is settled. Tomorrow, I will help Toby move his bed into the small room Anna currently sleeps in. He is too excited at having his own space to worry about the size. I do worry about him alone in there, but he can take care of himself, and the room is not big enough for a bed and the baby's crib both.

We just need to get through one more night.

March 13

I was permitted to accompany Father into town today. It was the first time I've seen other people in nearly two whole weeks. We shopped for supplies and Father asked around about work. I do hope he finds some soon, then I will have the house to myself in the daytime, at least. It would help my nerves, I think, though I've been somewhat less anxious since moving the baby into my bedroom.

It's peculiar, but several people very abruptly ended their conversations with us when they learned where we are living now. One of them, an old man, eyed me with such fear after hearing it that you'd think I was the devil himself. It made me uncomfortable, but less uncomfortable than the way I felt after being ogled by some of the men in the local tavern when we stopped for lunch.

I managed to ask Father about their peculiar behavior.

"Ghost stories," he said gruffly, brushing it off. I knew better than to ask again, but I can't help but think of the voices I heard last week. I've not heard anything since Toby switched rooms, so it's likely it was only my own fear and imagination making me hear things.

Still, I am glad Anna is nearby now. Though he misses Mother and he's still kind to me, Toby seems more like Father every day and it frightens me, what future might await him if he continues in this manner.

March 15

I had a queer encounter today.

I was out at the river, doing the laundry. One of the sheets got caught in the weeds, stuck on the sharp leaves of what the locals call "witch's hand." I yanked them free and turned around and found an old woman just behind me. It gave me a fright—I screamed out loud, then stepped back, embarrassed to be caught so off guard.

"Sorry to startle you, dear," she said.

"Oh no," I said. "I'm sorry to have shouted. I just didn't expect to see you there." I looked around, and it seemed as if there was nowhere she could have come from. The edge of the wood was the closest structure, aside from our house in the distance, and even that was too far away from such a frail old woman for her to have appeared so quickly.

But maybe I was distracted. Perhaps I didn't notice her approach. It was windy, and the wind blowing through the grasses caused a rustling that may have disguised her footsteps.

"That witch's hand will get you every time," the old woman said. "If you're gentle and patient, it should release easily. The more you fight it, the tighter its hold on you."

"Thank you," I said. "I'll keep that in mind for the future." I added, hesitant, "My name is Catherine. I live just over the other side of the river." I pointed out our house and the old woman made a soft sound of acknowledgement. "We moved in earlier this month."

"I noticed," the woman murmured. "I'm a neighbor. Gertrude. I live through the trees." She pointed to the edge of the woods. As far as I have noticed, those trees seem to go on forever. I don't know that I'd call anyone living on the other side of them a neighbor, but maybe things are different out here, so far from town.

"It's lovely to meet you, Gertrude," I said. "If you ever need anything, please don't hesitate to ask." I remembered Granny before she passed, the way her hands seized up and she needed help with everything. "I would be happy to help you, especially if you're all on your own."

"Sweet child," Gertrude said. She looked at me like ~~she could see into my soul she knew what I was thinking she was taking in my whole being~~

She looked at me oddly, then. But not unkindly.

"The same applies to you," she said. "Doubly, even. If there's ever anything you need—*anything*—just find your way into the trees. Once you're there, we'll be able to find you and help you."

Something about her words shook me to my core. I could feel the truth of them in my bones.

"'We?'" I asked. I felt foolish for thinking she must be on her own, just because I hadn't seen anyone else.

"My sisters and me," she said. "Just past the woods."

"I will keep that in mind," I said. "Thank you, Gertrude." I gestured towards the wet washing. "I should get this back over to the house, now, before my father makes a fuss, but it was lovely to meet you."

I picked up the laundry basket to go, and then suddenly there Gertrude was again. She held me by the wrists and looked directly into my eyes.

"I mean it, Catherine. *Anything.*"

Her eyes...I cannot describe what went through me, then. It was terrifying, but still I somehow felt. . .safe.

"Th-thank you," I stuttered in reply, and then quickly walked back towards the house.

I didn't turn around until I reached the washline, and once I did, she was gone.

I don't know what to make of this. I do not think she wished me harm, but the intensity and the fervor of her stare...there was something unsettling about her, despite the comfort that I felt in her presence.

I haven't told Father or Toby and I don't plan to.

March 19

Father took me into town again today. While he was talking to the grocer, the grocer's wife wandered over to make idle talk with me. She asked why we were in town and then asked after my mother. I told her that my mother disappeared some time ago and then Father took us to live here.

Father finished up his business quick and then grabbed my arm, hauling me out of the shop. He dragged me around the corner and slapped me hard across the face.

"Don't go telling anyone else our business, girl," he said. "Ever. You hear me?"

I nodded and he slapped me again.

"Say it!" he snapped.

"I won't," I managed to say, though I could feel my jaw swelling already, tender and purpling.

Sometimes I wish I could slap him back. Sometimes I wish he knew how it feels.

March 20

~~Today~~
~~I think that~~
~~I don't know~~

This evening, as I was getting the supper ready, Father went outside to tend to the horse.

I wasn't really thinking about it, but I glanced out the window as I prepared the vegetables, just in time to see

I'm not sure what I saw.

No, what I saw was one of the straps of the saddle, resting on the fence, come flying up and slap him on the cheek, just where he slapped me yesterday. Then, as he stood there, stunned, it did it again.

There was an evening breeze, but not nearly strong enough to move the leather strap of the saddle that far and that fast.

I gaped for but a moment and then quickly looked back to the vegetables, concentrating on the task. When he came in a few moments later, cheek red and starting to darken around the edges, I acted surprised.

"S'windy," was all he said as I tended to the wound.

Did I make this happen?

Is this my fault?

If I did make this happen, how can I stop it from happening again?

~~Do I want to stop it from happening again?~~

I don't think I'll be getting much sleep tonight.

March 23

I told myself when we moved to this town that I would do my best to put the past behind me and move forward. I thought, maybe, I might find someone who wanted to marry me and get out of my father's house once and for all. I thought, at the very least, I might make some friends.

It is hard to make friends here.

I am rarely let out. And now, the few instances when I can go into town, people are telling tales about me.

They're not about me, I suppose. They're about the house. The house we live in.

I met some boys and girls my age while Father was arguing with the man at the feed store. When I told them where I lived, they all went quiet.

"That's the witch house," one girl finally said.

"The witch house?" I asked.

"The women who live there, the house makes them witches," a boy said. "It takes their husbands and makes them witches."

I looked at them all again, waiting for them to say more, but they didn't. What's more, they wouldn't even look at me.

They made excuses to leave soon after, and the girl who called it a witch house stopped on the other side of the street, where she murmured something to another girl who looked at me with wide eyes, before both of them dashed away.

Only one girl lingered. She didn't say anything, but she looked at me for a long time. I was about to ask her name when Father reappeared and the girl ran off.

Finding time to talk to people my own age is hard enough with Father lingering over my shoulder, but now I just know that the whole town will know I live in the witch house by day's end. I'll never make friends. I'll never get away from this.

March 24

<u>Am I</u> becoming a witch?

March 31

Perhaps I was wrong about making friends! Oh, I hope I was wrong!

Today, while I was at the river doing the washing, I heard someone approach. Part of me expected it to be Gertrude again, but when I turned, it was the girl from the village last week. She also had a basket of laundry, but I knew there was a part of the river closer to the village where most of the girls and women do their washing work. It didn't make any sense that she would be so far upstream, unless . . .

Unless she had come especially to see me.

I was wary at first, afraid she had come to gawk at the girl turning into a witch, but she didn't keep her distance. She came right over to where I was washing.

"My name is Miriam," she said. "Do you mind if I wash up here?"

"No," I said faintly. "I'm Catherine." Then, more boldly, "I saw you in the village last week."

She smiled and nodded. It was a small, meek thing, but it was warm. I couldn't remember the last time someone had smiled so warmly at me.

"I don't go often, but my auntie encouraged it," she said. "I'm glad I went."

"I am too," I found myself saying, almost without realizing it.

We talked for a long time, much longer than it takes to do the washing. I learned that Miriam lives on the other side of the woods, same as Gertrude, the strange old woman from the other day. Miriam knows her, actually. "That's one of my aunties," she said, which made me feel more warmly towards Gertrude and Miriam both.

I told her a bit about my family, about Mother's disappearance and the move and being alone in the house all the time. I even told her a little about Father's temper. I was horrified to hear the words coming out of my mouth—

it is family business, I shouldn't be airing it to strangers—but she was so kind and compassionate. She was furious at Father, adamant that his temper isn't my fault, and as guilty as I feel, it was nice to have someone on my side, the way Mother used to be.

When we parted ways, she promised she would see me again soon. I hope she's right.

April 1

I am glad yesterday was a good day, because today was certainly a bad one.

I made Father's lunch as he left for his farm job, same as I do every morning. It was fine when I packed it away, but the food must have been on the cusp of spoiling, as it was all rotten by the time he opened it to eat.

It doesn't make any sense. The rest of the food here is fine. I tried to show that to him, tried to explain, but he didn't care.

My head is pounding from the blows and I've cleaned the blood as best I could, but I'm sure I look a sight.

I just pray that nothing goes wrong tomorrow and I have time to rest.

April 3

Today I went to the river and found Miriam there. She looked excited to see me, until she saw my face.

"What's happened to you?" she asked.

I told her about the strange issue with Father's lunch and the beating. She looked horrified and kept apologizing.

"It's not your fault," I insisted, and she went quiet and hugged me.

It had been a very long time since I had been hugged by anyone besides the baby.

It did not appear that she had any washing of her own to do, but she helped with mine, far more than I would have asked or expected. When it was all done, she said, "I would offer to carry it back for you, but I'm not supposed to cross the river."

It was an odd comment, but I certainly understood arbitrary rules. I thanked her again and I carried the wet clothes back to the house, feeling better despite the way my face still ached.

April 4

Today was strange.

Father has been having the wife of his employer make lunch for him since the incident last week with the rotten food. Today, it happened again—when he went to open his lunch, all of the food was spoiled rotten. It didn't happen to any of the other men, just him.

Very strange, but at least he couldn't blame it on me this time.

April 8

My days have been busy as of late. Anna is growing every day. She's teething and starting to move about and babble. Before long, she'll be crawling and talking.

I do honestly love to watch her grow. She's so beautifully happy and cheerful during the long days we spend together. ~~She is less happy and cheerful once Father and Toby return home.~~

It means I spend less time out of the house, however. I do the washing as quickly as I can manage, with Anna in tow, and haven't seen Miriam for more than a moment or two in days.

I miss her. I miss having someone, anyone to talk to. Toby is becoming gruff and distant the more time he spends in school, away from the family. I talk to Anna all day, but it's not as if she talks back.

I'm lonely.

April 9

This morning, as I was out tending to the garden, someone tapped me on the shoulder. I shrieked and jumped, but it was just Miriam, smiling cheerfully at me.

"I thought you weren't supposed to cross the river?" I asked, breathless.

"I'm not," she admitted. "But I missed you."

I missed her, too.

We didn't do anything of note, really. She helped me with my chores and entertained the baby while I did some of the more finicky cleaning that's difficult with an infant rolling around. We talked, mostly.

Still, it was the best day I've had in a while.

April 11

Miriam came by again today. Between the two of us, we managed to complete all the day's chores by lunch, so I made us a picnic and we took it out to the river.

Miriam seemed to relax the moment we crossed over the river to the clear spot on the bank where I normally do the laundry.

"You take not crossing the river seriously," I said.

She just nodded. "It's an old rule, but a fairly important one," she said. "But I'm happy to spend time with you." She leaned back and the wind blew the grass at the riverbank towards her. It looked like hands reaching out, and the way she gently stroked the stalk that came closest only enforced it.

"Gertrude called that Witch's Hand," I said.

"That's what we call it," Miriam confirmed. "If you fight its hold, it just gets worse, but be gentle and it will release you."

It was more or less what Gertrude said.

"A lot of people around here think of it as a nuisance, but it can protect you, too," Miriam continued. She looked over at me, her eyes dark and serious. They seemed endlessly deep and ancient in that moment. "Lots of things around here can protect you if you need it," she said softly. "The woods, for example. If anything happens—if you ever need anything—you can always run to the woods."

That, too, was what Gertrude said.

Before I could say that, or ask for more detail on what, precisely, she meant, Anna started gurgling for attention and Miriam looked away to find her a hard crust of bread to gnaw on.

All of these strange beliefs of Miriam's feel like they take on a greater importance when she's talking about them. I know they're all just local stories and tall tales, but they feel like . . . more.

April 15

Today, while Miriam and I were preparing lunch, Anna got up onto her hands and knees and took three wobbly movements towards us. Up until now, she's been pulling herself along the wooden floors with her hands, but today she actually crawled! It was delightful to see and wonderful to have someone with whom to share my delight.

Toby being distant, Father being angry...none of those things seems to matter as much when I'm alone with Anna and Miriam.

April 22

I haven't had much time to write. I haven't had much time to do anything. I've barely seen Miriam.

Father lost his job on the farm last week. In the days since, he's been stalking around the house and property and drinking far too much. I barely have a moment to myself and it's difficult to keep out of his way when he's this angry.

Sometimes at night I dream about running away to the woods with the baby. The dreams feel so real and I wake up desperately wishing they were.

April 26

Today, Father barked at me, "Go do something useful and take that screaming brat with you!"

It had been a hard morning and Anna's teeth were hurting her something awful. I didn't know what else to do, so I grabbed a blanket and a bottle and a toy for Anna and left the house. I went past the river and found a quiet place to sit down.

And then, just moments later ~~as if by magic~~, Miriam was there.

I hadn't realized just how much I missed her until I saw her. Something deep within me settled and relaxed for the first time in too many days.

I told her everything—about Father's unemployment, about his temple, about being stuck with him in the house.

"Well, you're not in the house now," she said. "And if he's going to continue to be so upset by the baby crying, maybe you can just...come out here in the afternoons?"

I don't know if it will work, if it will be that simple, but I think that maybe, if I time it right, if I wait until Anna kicks up a fuss, he won't think too hard about it.

He didn't think too hard about it today. I was home in time to make his dinner and he grunted in acknowledgement when we came in, but otherwise didn't say a word. He'd had too much to drink, by that point, to notice much of anything.

I'll try again tomorrow, I think. Maybe this time, I'll pack a lunch in advance.

April 29

This marks two months that we've been here and eight since Mother disappeared.

At least I have Anna and Miriam. Father has not yet commented on the way the baby and I disappear in the afternoons. I think he's just relieved to not have to deal with us.

April 30

~~I don't know~~
~~I can't believe I've been so fool~~
~~I knew it couldn't last~~
~~I don't understand why~~
Today, I stayed out later than I should have. Dinner was still on the table in time, but I had to rush just a bit to ensure it.

Father noticed.

He noticed when I came in late and he noticed how I had to rush through dinner preparation in order to have a meal ready for the family.

"What do you do out in those fields all day, anyway?" he asked, eyes narrowed.

"Nothing!"

I was too quick to answer. I know that now. I should have stayed calm and brushed off the question, pretended it didn't matter. But I couldn't. I was so seized with fear that I spoke without thinking and it only made him more suspicious.

He didn't respond, but I could tell from the way he was looking at me that I hadn't quite convinced him of anything.

I don't know what I'll do if this outlet is taken from me, if I have to give up my time with Miriam and stay instead in the house with him all day. The very thought brings tears to my eyes.

I shouldn't go out there tomorrow. I should stay close to home until his suspicions fade. I just wish I had a way to tell Miriam that it isn't her fault.

May 1

~~No no no no no no no no no~~
~~It's all my fault~~

I am writing quickly and I apologize to whoever reads this, but I'm not sure how much time I have.

This afternoon, I meant only to run out to explain to Miriam why I wouldn't be around any longer. I waited until Father was distracted, but maybe he wasn't as distracted as I thought. I had been with Miriam for only a few moments, explaining what had happened as Anna crawled at my feet, when Father was suddenly upon us.

He was angry. He was drunk. He was yelling so loudly I could barely make out his words. He took a swing at me that I ducked, and then he

Then he tried to hurt Anna.

I can't let her end up like me. I can't let him hurt her.

I took her and I ran. I took the most twisted path back to the house that I could manage, but it's only a matter of time before he returns and finds us.

I don't know what to do.

I don't know what

I'm in the woods.

It's dark here and I don't know where I am, but I also feel like I'm...safe. I'm still scared.

When Father came back to the house, I still didn't know what to do, until my mind fell back on what Miriam had said, what Gertrude had said. The memory was so sharp that it was like someone was whispering the words into my ear. "Come to the woods."

But it was just a memory. It had to be.

I threw some clothes and this journal and a doll and Anna's bottle into a sack and managed to get the sack, the baby, and myself out the window while my father was still banging against my bedroom door.

Toby spotted us before we got far. He shouted for Father and then both of them were chasing us. I had a head start, but barely, and they're both much faster than I am, but as we got close to the river, they seemed to slow. The Witch's Hand was tangled in their pant cuffs and they couldn't seem to get loose, no matter how hard they struggled.

I didn't look for long. I kept running, sure that at any moment they would get free and be upon me.

I ran all the way to the woods, Anna screaming the whole time. I was so terrified that her cries would give us away. I kept running into the woods, but they were thicker and darker than I would have thought. Finally, I came upon a hollowed out tree, and that's where I am writing this now.

The tree is oddly warm and the baby has finally stopped crying. She's calm and quiet where I hold her on my lap. I've caught my breath and the urgency seems to have evaporated, even though I'm sure that Father and Toby are still in pursuit.

That feeling of safety is heavy and thick, though. I feel like they can't find me here, even though I know that's impossible.

But maybe it's not. I can hear singing, women singing, further into the trees. I swear I can hear Miriam's voice among them, and the melody is welcoming. Warm.

I know I have to go to them, from the same place deep within me that I knew I had to get to the woods, that I would be safe once I got here.

That maybe, here, I'll be safe forever.

Anna is quiet, and I think I can see a warm glow coming from the trees further ahead. I think it's time to seek it out.

I think it's time to join them.

The Woods

Christine Ricketts

No one goes into the woods anymore.

They'll look to it, scowl at it, peer into the dark undergrowth, but they won't go in. Even the bravest and boldest of the towns-folk turn their backs to it and pretend like the long stretch of looming trees isn't even there.

Just like they'll talk about the woman who lives within; they'll gossip, or curse, or cross themselves in fear without ever speaking her name.

Hag's got her hand in that no doubt.

Hag's hand touched that one all right.

And even quieter, they'll murmur their grudging need.

That'll need the hag's hand, else it won't mend right.

Crops've withered, hag ain't been by lately.

No one goes into the woods.

But when things are dire and grim, when murmurs become whispers and desperation has no other avenue to travel, something comes *out* of the woods. Only at night when the sky is so black it seems that the stars have all gone out, riding along on rumors and hearsay. On wings, on a broomstick, in a carved stone pestle.

However it travels, it comes.

Illness is pushed aside, the unfortunate seen to, the rain delivered or the snow delayed.

The hag's given her hand.

We should take the hag's head, end the curses before they even begin.

Some men in the village don't whisper or murmur. They look to the woods and spit, sharpen their tools and their courage but still they won't enter the woods.

The woods are dark in full daylight, the trees thick and full. Even in the dead of winter the canopy is heavy and green under the white blanket of snow.

Should just burn it down around the hag. A proper pyre for a witch, those men argue. Attack the beast from the outside, no need to draw in close.

There's good timber, the others protest though no one has ever cut down a tree in living memory.

The woods are cursed. Leave 'em be.

The whole town's cursed.

But no one enters the woods.

Ellie stood at the edge of the woods. Behind her heard the distinct sounds of the town waking up. Farm animals and the distant chatter of voices as chores were tended to. Ahead through the trees, there was nothing. Not the twittering of birds or the rustle of leaves. Just silence.

No one went into the woods.

She knew even though no one had ever specifically *told* her that. No one had ever looked at her and said *Ellie, now girl, don't you step foot in those woods, do you hear me?* Not her Ma or Pa or even her older brother Thom. They all just moved around it like everyone else in the town, avoiding it as if it weren't even there.

Except when they needed something. Then they would look, just out of the corner of their eyes, as they spoke, just out of the corner of their mouths. Like when Old Man Sanders' cows had all been sick and dried up. Or when more than a month had gone by without rain. They'd looked and they'd whispered and the cows had started milking again and the rain had come.

And then they all went right back to not looking and not talking.

Well. Ellie needed something, too. And no amount of looking at the woods had fixed what she *knew* needed fixing.

So, Ellie went into the woods.

It felt like she walked for *hours*. There was no path, no clear route through the closely spaced trees and only thin tendrils of sunlight streamed down from overhead. Ellie walked and heard only the rustle of her own footsteps—the shuffling sound was poor company.

Suddenly, like a great mouth opening wide, the trees gave way to a clearing. In the center of the space sat the strangest hut she had ever seen— circular rather than square like the ones in her village. The roof gleamed like copper just smelted and a crooked chimney poked out from the center. There were windows cut in strange shapes and plants of all kinds growing between the wooden panels.

But strangest of all was the fact that it sat up in the air, nearly ten feet or so, held up by two scrawny chicken legs.

Ellie wondered if that was what the townsfolk were looking for when they looked to the woods. Or was it what was in the hut? For the first time since she entered the woods, Ellie felt a prickle of fear in the pit of her stomach.

After all, no one goes into the woods.

Though she tried to tell her feet to turn back she found herself cautiously creeping forward. Her eyes darted to each window, wondering if she was really seeing dark shapes within or if it was just a trick of her imagination.

Before she realized it Ellie had inched her way all the way up to the front door. It loomed well above her head and out of reach. Up close the chicken legs looked even skinnier and she could not see how they connected to the house itself. Was the inside a giant chicken that had grown too big for the house and simply pushed through the floor?

She was just about to duck her head beneath the hut for a closer look when a raspy voice called out,

"Never lost, never found, put my house on solid ground."

Ellie stumbled back just in time before the two bird legs folded in and the house dropped to the ground with a quiet *thump*. The door swung open and a large old woman with lumpy features and long fingers stood in the doorway. She peered out with wide, watery eyes from beneath a thick wool shawl. When her gaze landed on Ellie the girl was startled by the vivid blue color. The old woman smiled with surprisingly strong looking teeth and her large shoulders curled up towards drooping ears.

"Ah, a visitor comes to see Baba Yaga. Come, come in child, and tell me what you've come for."

Ellie found that she could not look away from those blue eyes but took a step backward nonetheless. She had heard the story of the old woman who baked children into bread.

As if she had said the words out loud Baba Yaga cackled, waving one spindly arm and leaning down so that her face was only a few inches away.

"Come come now, you're safe. I've already had my bread today child."

Swallowing her fear Ellie stepped inside the hut.

The interior of the house was just as odd as the outside. The single room was spacious, far larger than seemed possible and bits and bobbins hung from every single inch. A massive fireplace took up most of one wall and a heavy black cauldron hung over the fire. On a wooden stand in front of it three crows chattered at each other. They grew silent when Ellie entered.

"You are from the village near the edge of the woods, yes?"

Ellie nodded automatically and then blinked. "But how did you know that?"

The crone continued to smile as she shuffled to a large cabinet, drawing the doors open. Shelves lined with curiosities greeted her, a few literally. With a quick hand, she smacked what looked like a small box that rushed forward on four legs back into the recesses of the cupboard.

"I know many things, child."

Baba Yaga's eyes were so big and so wide that Ellie thought she must see everything.

"My mother is sick. She needs help," Ellie heard herself say.

Baba Yaga slunk from the cabinet to the cauldron, her knobby fingers full of roots, moss, and jars that clinked together.

"Then why have you come to me?" she prompted.

Ellie stared at the old woman. "Because you fix things. You could make her better."

A small cloud of smoke puffed up from the cauldron as Baba Yaga began to sift the ingredients in her hands into the pot. Ellie watched mesmerized as the smoke shifted colors; dark blue, blood red, deep purple.

"Has the doctor seen her?"

Ellie nodded.

"And why do you think I could help if the doctor could not?"

"Because you're a witch!" Ellie blurted out. She bit her lip and dropped her gaze to the floor but couldn't help but add, "And you know magic. You can make the rain come and the cows give milk. You can make her well again."

There was silence, long and deep, and Ellie wondered if the old woman had left the room. She couldn't bring herself to raise her head to see. Her chest hurt, right in the center, where her mother would rest her hand whenever Ellie herself was sick.

"Do you know what magic is, child?"

Ellie nodded again. "It's spells and chants and potions."

There was a quiet chuckle and Ellie felt something pressed into her hands. Lifting her eyes, she saw it was a cup of swirling liquid, somehow all the colors that she had seen in the smoke only a moment ago.

"Only to those that don't know any better."

"Then what is it really?"

"It's knowing how the winds shift and which plants make the cows ill. That the way things are, aren't the way things will always be."

A firm pressure under her chin tipped Ellie's chin up and she found herself staring once more into Baba Yaga's fathomless eyes.

"It's patience. And acceptance."

"I don't want my mom to die," Ellie whispered and the pain in her chest grew.

"No, I reckon you don't."

"Will you help me?"

The deep lines of Baba Yaga's face tightened and for a moment Ellie thought she had made the old woman angry. But then the crone was suddenly shuffling away, back to the smoking cauldron where she drew a long ladle and poured steaming liquid into a squat ceramic jar. She pressed a seal of wax over the lid and handed it to Ellie.

"If your mother can drink this for three days then she'll recover. But she must drink *only* this and nothing else."

Ellie took the jar carefully, feeling the warmth through the smooth material. The pain in her chest receded and she beamed up at the old woman.

"Thank you! Thank you so much!"

She ran toward the door but paused at the threshold. Looking back over her shoulder, she said, "I haven't anything to pay you with."

"Come back and visit me, if your mother recovers," the hag stated.

Ellie frowned. "What if she doesn't recover?"

"Come back anyway."

The journey back was far shorter than Ellie expected, even though she walked slowly with the jar cradled close to her body so as not to drop it.

At home she found her father hunched over his ledger book, his face gaunt and weary. He looked up when she entered and smiled tiredly though he did not ask where she had been.

"How is she?" Ellie asked, holding the jar behind her back.

"Tired," he said, as he always did. His eyes shifted to the door to their bedroom. "The day was hard for her."

"I'll take her some tea before bed," Ellie offered, shifting toward the kitchen, careful to keep her body turned. Her father looked as if he might object and then sighed.

"All right. But don't tarry long. She needs her rest."

Ellie nodded and slipped past him, excitement racing through her. She pulled down her mother's squat tea mug, the one that Ellie had helped her make and carried it to the bedroom, pushing the door open as quietly as she could manage.

It was dark with the curtains drawn tight but she could still see the faint shape of her mother lying bundled on the bed. She crept over and set the mug onto the small table near the bed. It took no time at all to peel back the wax and she poured the tonic from Baba Yaga into the cup. For a moment she could still see the glowing colors that had risen from the smoking cauldron. And then the liquid swirled and grew dark as steeped tea. She could see tendrils of heat still rising.

"Ellie?" Her mother's voice, weak and raspy, drifted out and the bundle of blankets turned over. "Ellie, is that you?"

"Yes, mama. I brought you some tea."

"Oh, that's nice honey. I don't think I can drink anything right now."

"I made it special for you. It'll help make you feel better."

She heard her mother sigh and one thin hand snuck out from underneath the blankets.

"Well then, perhaps just a bit."

For three days Ellie tended to her mother, bringing food and drink into the room but never letting anything but the potion pass her mother's lips.

And each day her mother grew sicker and weaker. By the second day she could no longer lift the mug herself and needed Ellie to guide her shaking hands.

By the third day it was Ellie's hands alone that held the cup.

On the morning of the fourth day there was no more potion to give. So, Ellie went to make a regular cup of tea instead. Her father and the doctor had been up late speaking in hushed tones and the door to her mother's bedroom was closed. There were no sounds of stirring behind it. She wondered if her father had already risen and gone out for the morning chores but noticed that his boots were still near the front door.

She hung the kettle over the fire to boil and took down her mother's jar of tea. As she measured out the portion, she noticed a thick black substance clinging to the dried leaves. She lifted the spoon to look closer and an awful smell had her twisting away. She dumped the mixture back into the jar and took it outside, shaking it out into the dirt. To her disgust a pair of spiders skittered away, disappearing into the grass.

Ellie stared down at the jar. Her mother had always taken tea in the evenings before she had gotten sick. Furrowing her brow, Ellie tried to recall the last time she had bought a new batch from the shop in town. It had been quite a while, since money was tight. And when money was tight, sometimes her mother would supplement her tea with leaves picked near the stream.

Slowly Ellie lifted her eyes to the edge of the woods.

"Ellie? Ellie, come here now," her father called.

The trip through the woods was shorter this time. When Ellie entered the clearing, the hut was already seated and the curling form of Baba Yaga was picking through the plants hanging from her windows. She watched Ellie's approach without pausing her work.

"Can you teach me?" Ellie asked when she drew close enough.

Baba Yaga wrinkled her nose. "And how is your mother, child?"

"The doctor says she's on the mend. Can you teach me?" Ellie repeated.

"I could. But you've already learned."

"I want to learn more."

"That we can do, then."

PART III

Oracle

a priest or priestess acting as a medium through whom advice or prophecy was sought from the gods in classical antiquity.

Elegy for Spent Sweat

Lara Eckener

I. You remember being young, building castles on this coarse black sand. You remember the midnight horizon of dark coming to rest against dark, obscuring the distance between you and forever. This was before you learned the word fate, before you knew parapets were for jumping from as surely as they were for watching from, before you knew benevolence was only ever a god with his own agenda. Just because you feel touched by beauty does not mean the beauty is there to serve you. It begins and it ends here at the sea.

All of the salt you shed between birth and death will make you cousin to the waves.

II. The slender road down to the water has been thickly covered over with flowers—like your slender wrists, ankles, and throat—meant to cover over the signs that there are ever tired, hungry, desirous, monotonous human lives moving along these arteries. They have hidden your veins, but not veiled your tears, and you wish that this could be a private moment of grief between you and your new sisters, but you are Chosen and nothing you do will ever again be for yourself. As you shove the body along, you trip and fall to your knees, are dragged a short way, find the stone beneath the petals. You are being recorded by a thousand phones, a hundred tape recorders, ten or so pads of paper. Later it will all be transferred to canvases and screens. It is the only prophecy they will ever collect from you that they will be able to share without shame or fear, without opening themselves up to scrutiny. Here they have to open only you.

This is your first act. The wind is cold, it smells of salt, and you are burying yourself.

III. The three of you push the funerary sled down to the water's edge: the Oracle of Glass Tears, the Oracle of Blood in the Water, the Oracle of Spent Sweat. The last is you, with your hands on the sled, and again, inside of the sled. The dead girl does not have your face, and you do not have her power, but you are tied together. Two bodies, one meaning, you mourn yourself for everyone to see.

As soon as the water starts to lap at the flowers in her hair, the clock starts on the rest of your life.

IV. Once the sled and the girl are buoyant in the waves, the Oracle of Glass Tears and the Oracle of Blood in the Water sink to their knees. The frenzied white waves push against their chests and they sway with the movement, as well as against the weight of their tide-pulled gold and scarlet silks reaching back for the road, desperate to return to the shore. They let out a wailing you did not know could come from such fragile bird-like chests. They are grieving hands and lips, eyes and warm skin, and all of the unnamed intimacies that find people in the night. You don't know what those are, but you will, and your bird-like chest burns with the commingling fear and desire of precognition.

There is nothing in you that will not bleed from seven billion similarly pricked bodies.

V. There is violence in letting go. The Oracle of Glass Tears cries jagged, delicately etched memories into the water, rubbing her skin raw by tugging at her cheeks and eyelids to give the shards an easier birth. The Oracle of Blood in the Water cuts a deep line beneath each eye and squeezes out blood with the tears. This is the third line down each cheek and you know she will be the one you mourn next. It is cold, and you did not break a sweat coming down the road, so you begin your offering with a dance—a frenzied heaving of yourself through the water. The droplets begin to steam away, leaving behind the salt. The bystanders watch in silence, your only music the sounds of two women wailing, gone sotto voce as their voices are whipped away by the wind. This first ritual is an honor and a lesson.

It takes three to scry because no one person can be trusted with the future, especially not their own.

VI. The waves wash the flowers away from your wrists, from the shore, from your neck, from her hair. You cannot use the past to divine the future, because time is not a line. Time is a miscommunication the gods never bothered to set right. They became enamored with the feeling of taking young women by the chin, of lifting their faces to the sky, of saying *You owe me your beauty for your life.* Such a small price, such a small benevolence.

Once her body has been claimed there will be nothing left to bind you but the salt.

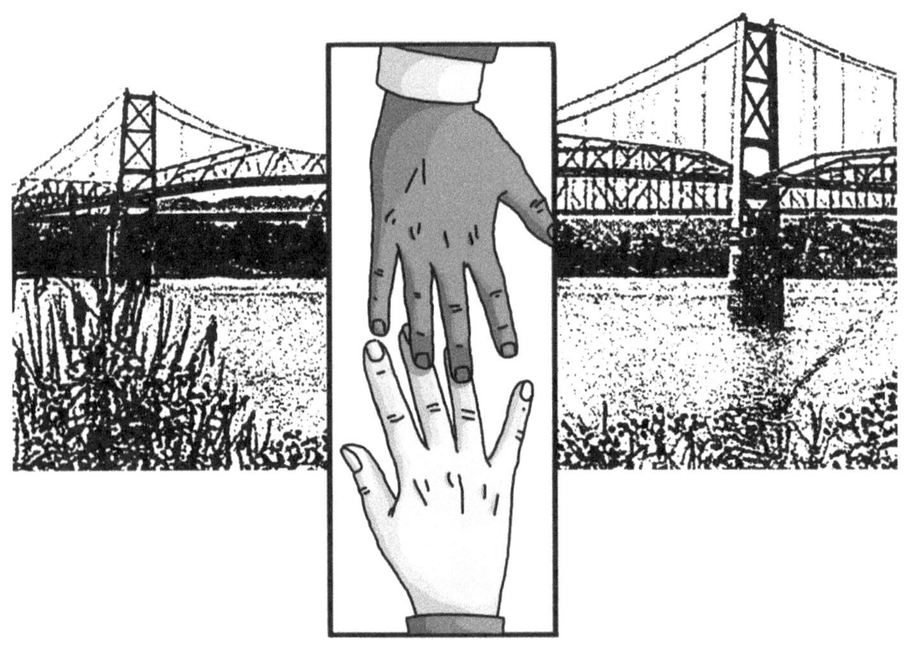

Damned If You Do

Kaitlyn Sudol

The bridge goes down, and Indrid Cold wakes up.

The image lingers, reverberating into his conscious mind from the wispy dream where it appeared to him. The bridge goes down. Vehicles crash into the icy water below. Humans screaming. Humans dying.

It's not the first vision that Indrid has received in his very long life. It won't be the last. He's dreamed of regimes falling and read about their demise in the newspaper months later. He's dreamed of nameless deaths and outbreaks of disease long before they happened. He's dreamed of war and famine that he later watched play out on the world stage.

This feels different, somehow.

He sits at the small, bare table in his small, bare room and opens his sketchbook, drawing the bridge with sharp, sure lines until the picture on the page matches the picture in his head.

He stares at it for a long time, then pins it to the wall next to his bed and tries to put it from his mind.

Indrid can pass for human. He's a little too tall and a little too thin, but with a heavy coat and slumped shoulders, no one gives him a second glance. That doesn't mean he should associate with humans. He shouldn't. He knows that. And he doesn't.

Usually.

There's a small cafe in town. They sell freshly squeezed lemonade and it's nearly always busy enough that he blends into the background, but not busy enough that they're in a rush to get him out the door. He can linger and sip his drink and eavesdrop on the humans flowing in and out of the shop. It's a simple way to keep abreast of world and local news and to keep himself up to date on local slang and mannerisms. It helps him fit in.

It's also a place he can meet John.

Back in late winter, John almost hit Indrid with his van. Indrid's fault—he'd been caught up in a premonition and wandered into the road. John left his van to see if Indrid was all right and instead of flying away, like he should have, or keeping his human form and dashing into the woods, he allowed John to speak with him for several minutes.

It was reckless, but John is fascinating and kind and Indrid had seen his face before in too many premonitions to count.

"We'll speak again soon," Indrid had said before waving farewell and retreating back into the woods. He hadn't necessarily meant for it to be true, but when he dreamt of John a few nights later, he found himself following the patchy images in his mind to a bench by a small pond.

"You weren't wrong about speaking again," John said. Then, "I thought I dreamed you."

"I did dream you," Indrid said. He knew, once the words left his mouth, that he should have held them back. Premonitions never seemed to apply to anything practical.

But John just smiled and gestured for Indrid to sit down next to him. "Let's talk, then," he said.

Months have passed. Sometimes they meet by the pond and sometimes Indrid calls him from a payphone, but most frequently they meet here. John works next door, and no one asks too many questions.

"You look preoccupied," John says today.

"I had strange dreams," Indrid says.

"Hopefully they weren't about another sewing machine repairman that you're going to go talk to instead," John says with a sly grin. Indrid grins back automatically. He knows his smile isn't quite right, but John has never complained.

"No, they weren't," Indrid says. He wants to say, *I wouldn't go to him even if they were*, but that feels like crossing a line that he doesn't dare approach. Talking to a normal human regularly is bad enough—he doesn't know what will happen if he allows himself to be pulled down much deeper. "Just. . .strange."

"Hm," John says. He moves his hand to lie on the table and his fingers just brush up against Indrid's. The room, briefly, seems to spin about them. "Could they be about your mysterious past? We've been talking for months and I still don't know anything about you, you know."

"Not the past," Indrid says. He's steadily watching the place where John's fingers overlap his own.

"Present?" John cocks his head to the side and smiles again. "Future?"

Indrid was expecting that, so he doesn't react or draw his hand away guiltily, the way he might have otherwise. John traces the tip of his finger along the tips of Indrid's fingers and Indrid ignores the future and pretends he doesn't know what that means.

"It was...I saw a bridge collapse," Indrid says, because seeing the future doesn't mean he's any better at holding conversations even when he's not flustered. "In my dream. There were people on it. Cars. Everyone died."

John abruptly stops the trail of his fingertip along Indrid's knuckles and freezes, his little smile melting into a frown.

"Oh jeez, that's horrible," he says. He retracts his hand. "No wonder you're preoccupied."

Indrid wants to reach across the table and take John's hand in his own. He wants to tell John that it's no matter, that he's seen worse. He wants to ask John what he dreams about.

"I suppose," Indrid says. "I'm sorry I'm poor company today."

"You're never poor company, Indrid Cold," John says, and the smile, at least, reappears.

Once upon a time, Indrid had family. He was surrounded by others like him. There were rules and a society. But he's the only one on this planet, now, and the rules are easy to bend and twist. It's easy to walk among humans for more than just supplies and emergencies. It's easy to add creature comforts to his little house—books, soft things, a radio. Small indiscretions, really, a reed bowing in the wind. He hasn't broken any of the biggest rules yet. He hasn't committed any crimes against his people. All of this has been done in the name of fitting in, of blending in.

These are the things he tells himself.

It's okay to enjoy a sweet drink on a hot day. It's okay to listen to music in the quiet evenings on his own. It's okay to grow attached to the world.

It's okay to say "yes" when John begs him to come out to the lake one evening, just as the sun is setting.

"You're so strange, Indrid," John says to him as they sit side-by-side on the dock. The lake is deserted, save for the lighted houses far on the other side. "I can never read you. I can never be sure what you want."

"What I want is inconsequential," Indrid says quietly.

"Well, that's silly," John says. "Of course it's of consequence. All we are is our choices. All we are is what we want."

Indrid has been dreaming of the bridge for weeks.

"You and I have very different relationships with fate," Indrid says.

John looks almost annoyed at that. He purses his lips and looks at Indrid thoughtfully.

"Oh," Indrid murmurs as the vision hits him seconds before the reality—John leaning in and pressing their lips together. He's still not ready for it when it happens, nor is he ready for John's hands on his face, holding him steady, or the way his heart jumps into his throat.

It's a short but thorough kiss. It's not shy, even when John slowly pulls back, head tilted, looking a little abashed.

"I don't even know if that's what you wanted," he admits. Then he adds, "It's what I wanted. To be clear."

Indrid tries not to let himself think about the things he wants, so he's surprised at how quickly, how seamlessly he draws John back to him and kisses him again.

He can almost hear the *snap* of the rules breaking for good.

Summer turns to fall. Indrid dreams of floods and elections. He dreams of assassinations and space. He dreams of the bridge, the bridge, the bridge.

He doesn't know why the bridge is special. He doesn't even know what bridge it is. It's not a large bridge, to be certain—the back drop isn't Manhattan or San Francisco. It's a small bridge. It's old. Parts are wearing out.

He wonders if maybe that's the reason he can't stop thinking about it, can't stop drawing it. He can't stop torrential rains or public murders. He can't turn the tide of war. But one bridge? One small bridge is something that he could save, maybe. One small bridge is in his power to protect.

The rules are gone now, after all. John spends night after night in Indrid's little cabin, sharing his little bed. The rules are far behind him.

"It's strange," John says one night, his hand resting on Indrid's chest. If he notices Indrid's irregular heartbeat, he hasn't mentioned it so far. "I feel like I know nothing and everything about you. It's so contradictory, but I don't know how else to explain it."

"You know me better than anyone else on this planet," Indrid replies. It's the sad truth. He's the only one left on Earth.

And if he's the only one left on Earth, what do the rules matter? The rules were created to shape a society. There is no society any longer. There is no colony. There's just Indrid, alone in the woods, with a gentle young human who brings him small gifts and looks at him with an affection that shakes Indrid down to his furthest depths.

And that's how the trouble starts.

It's early on a Saturday and John arrives with sweets from the cafe while Indrid is sitting at the table, sketching. It's the bridge again; he keeps futilely hoping that if he gets it down on paper, he'll get it out of his head. It hasn't worked so far, but he's not sure what else to do, at this point.

"Good morning." John presses a kiss to Indrid's cheek, a small burst of warmth to which he still isn't acclimated. "I've brought some muffins and that lemon cake that you like."

Indrid is still in the clothes he wears to sleep in this form. He hasn't even put the kettle on yet. He woke up and thought *bridge, bridge, bridge* and sat down to sketch. He's lucky that he wasn't in his other form, but, if he's being honest with himself, he rarely is these days. There's always the chance that John will pop in unexpectedly, and, beyond that, there's something comfortable about this visage. When he was younger, he far preferred his other form. It was freeing, the knowledge that he could take off at any moment, go above, *away* from the chaos of life on the ground.

Things change. All too quickly, as Indrid knows.

"That's very kind of you," Indrid says. He gets up from the table to start putting away his paper and pencils, his pile of sketches, but John's fingers drift over the smudged pencil of his latest drawing of the bridge.

"The Silver Bridge," he says faintly. "You sure do like that bridge, huh? You've got one up on the wall, too."

Time seems to stop, or maybe it's just that the blood rushing past Indrid's ears drowns out the ambient noise of the world moving around them. Indrid swallows and then places his hand over John's to keep it in place, poised over the bridge.

"Do you know what bridge this is?" he asks, slow and measured.

John nods. He's looking at Indrid as if Indrid has lost his mind. It's probably a testament to how accommodating John is that Indrid hasn't seen this look very frequently in the past.

"It's the Silver Bridge," he says again. "It's up the river in Point Pleasant. An hour or so by car. Surely you must have seen it before, these drawings are perfect."

"I must have seen it in the paper at some point," Indrid says, dazed. "It's just. . .in my head."

Just up the river. This bridge is just up the river. This bridge that's due to collapse on some snowy night is just up the river.

"Indrid...?" John twists his hand within Indrid's grip so he can weave their fingers together and gently squeeze Indrid's hand.

"Sorry," Indrid says. He shakes his head clear. "Sorry, I—I'm surprised."

"Okay," John says. "Are you all right?"

Indrid nods and then releases John's hand. "Yes, I'm—I'm fine. Have a seat. I'll change. I'll. . .put on the kettle."

John is still frowning. He strokes Indrid's cheek with the back of his fingers and Indrid tries not to shiver. He doesn't say anything else, however, and after a moment, Indrid gently steps away and into the corner to change his clothes.

They fall into a silence that's closer to normal as Indrid puts the kettle on and adds some wood to his stove in hopes of warming up the cabin. John retrieves a plate from Indrid's meagerly stocked cupboard and places an array of treats onto it. Before long, they're sitting together, sipping tea and sharing a muffin. Beneath the table, John's ankle is hooked around Indrid's.

Indrid is trying to focus on John's company and not the fact that the bridge might as well be in his backyard.

"You're so quiet," John says. "You're normally quiet—I wish you'd talk more—but you're extra quiet today. I can tell there's something on your mind."

"There is," Indrid admits.

He's sitting here in his little house, filled with his things, sharing a meal with a human who has become his lover. What's the point of following the few rules that he hasn't already shattered?

"If you could see the future. . .if you could know that something bad is going to happen. . .would you stop it?" Indrid asks.

John opens his mouth to respond and then closes it, staring thoughtfully into space.

"I think I would," he says eventually. He turns to Indrid. "That was my gut reaction—that I would, of course, stop something terrible from happening if it was in my purview. But I suppose seeing the future would be different, wouldn't it? You know that this is how something is going to happen, and disrupting it might derail the course of events."

John has just neatly expressed an idea that it took some children who grew up with Indrid years to comprehend.

"Still," John continues, "I don't know that I could stand to have something terrible on my conscience like that. How would you live with such a thing?"

Easily, Indrid doesn't say. He's lost no sleep over the atrocities of man and the wrath of nature.

But that's not entirely true. Because he's been losing sleep over the bridge.

"It's hard to understand what we can live with until we experience it," Indrid replies.

"I suppose that's true," John says. "It doesn't change my answer, though. If I knew something terrible was happening and it was in my ability to stop it, I would. I don't think I'd like the person I would be if I did otherwise."

Indrid isn't sure he's ever liked who he is. He isn't sure he's ever even thought about it before. He isn't sure that he wants to start.

When John leaves, Indrid bundles up and slips into town. He buys a road map at the general store and manages to procure a phone book. He takes both back to the cabin and pins the map up on the wall near the drawing of the bridge.

He traces the route from his cabin to the Silver Bridge. It's a meandering drive along the river.

It would be a quick flight, though.

He's surprised that it takes some thinking to remember when he last took flight. Late at night, close to the trees, he would let himself get lost in the freedom of movement. It didn't matter that he was alone and it didn't matter that he had no purpose. He could put his mind to rest and focus only on the wind whipping past him and the movement of his wings. It's been months since he went flying, weeks since he even thought about it.

He glances over to make sure the door is locked and closes the drapes, then shifts right there in the middle of the kitchen. It's like standing up after too long at rest in a cramped space. He feels his joints pop and his muscles burn. He moves his wings up and down once, fluttering the map on the wall and the pile of drawings on the small table near his bed. He stretches to alleviate the soreness all over his body, and wonders how he reached a point where this form feels so foreign. He stares down at his hands, dark as night and longer, narrower. He wonders when he began to think of this form as monstrous.

He wonders what John would say if he were to walk in right now.

Indrid shifts back to his other form and rolls his shoulders. He looks again at the map on the wall and traces the best route from here to Point Pleasant. When he's sure he knows where he's going, he sits at the table and waits for midnight. After the last of the light fades into the evening and the clock ticks down to the end of the day, he takes a deep breath and goes outside.

It's already cold outside. Indrid, who is frequently cold even during the longest days of summer, shivers violently in the gloom. He looks around quickly and, satisfied that no one is watching, he shifts forms again. There's more room to stretch out here—he flaps his wings several times in rapid succession and stretches them out, arches his feet until he's standing fully on his toes. He's taller this way and his night vision is better. He can hear every sound in the forest around him.

This is the way he was meant to be, but it still feels like he's playing pretend.

He launches himself into the air and takes off down the path he's traced for himself. He follows the river, keeping close to the trees and avoiding the glowing lights from the houses he sees sprinkled across the land below. The wind is cold, but it makes his lungs feel larger, like he's only now getting a full breath after too long without.

It's a beautiful flight. It makes him think of John, though he can't understand why.

When he gets close to Point Pleasant, he nearly stops flying mid-air. Before him is the bridge he's been dreaming about for months. It's lit up like a beacon in the dark, and Indrid's mind overlays the destruction as he stares at it.

All this time and it was right down the river.

He slows, moving carefully along the edge of town and then skirting inside of it. Most houses are dark, but he sticks to the shadows until he can't any longer, then says a quiet prayer to a long dead god and takes flight once again, racing to the base of the bridge.

He finds a perch on the underside of the bridge and then pauses. What does he do now? He peers at various findings and components, but he doesn't know anything about bridge construction. The metal seems rusted and the wood weathered, but he doesn't know how that affects structural integrity. He can see the bridge's collapse in his mind's eye, but it gives him little insight into how he can stop it.

He flies from perch to perch beneath the bridge, studying it. He hopes that there will be something obvious—a twisted beam, a missing bolt—but nothing sticks out. When he's looped around the entire underside, he stops to regroup. It's easy to feel dismayed and discouraged, but he came out here without a plan. He doesn't know exactly when the bridge will fall, but he knows there will be snow on the ground. That gives him another month or two at least, if not longer. He has time to think about this predicament and figure out how to handle it. He can still save this bridge, he just needs to focus.

He flies back home and lands, exhausted, not long before dawn. He barely takes a moment to change back into his other form and then crawls naked into his bed.

He doesn't dream about the bridge.

Indrid spends Sunday pacing and considering his options. John is absent, at church with his family and then off to his grandmother's house, so Indrid starts the morning in his other form, shifting back to his more human shape after a few hours. He tells himself it's for convenience—it's easier to move around in the house if he's human-sized—but he can't ignore the way his skin starts to prickle uncomfortably the more time he spends as a monster.

He can't ignore that he thinks of that form as monstrous now.

By Monday morning, he has something resembling a plan. He makes his way to the library in town and hunts down the few texts on bridges and engineering that are available on the shelves. He reads about bridge construction and analyzes his memory of the premonition as deeply as he can to pinpoint where the collapse occurs. He asks the library for copies of information on the building of the Silver Bridge. He reads through articles and history. He takes notes.

At the end of the day, he returns home and reads through his papers until late into the night. When it's nearly midnight, he flies back to Point Pleasant.

He's able to enjoy the flight more this time. He knows where he's going and the best way to get there. He has a concrete plan. He looks out over the countryside as he passes it by, marveling at all of the people living their lives below, unaware of how close they're inching to disaster.

Unless he can stop it. If nothing else, he has to try.

Unfortunately, even with all his new research, finding any structural problems with the bridge is difficult. He focuses on the Ohio side, near where the first part of the collapse happens in his mind, but he needs to be circumspect and it's hard to tell if any parts are deficient. He studies the eyebars one at a time, studies the joints in the chain, but everything seems solid. There are no glaring issues and while everything looks older and worn, nothing appears dangerously thin or off-kilter. He knows that something happens on this one portion of the bridge that causes the whole thing to go down in less than a minute. He has no idea where it starts or why.

It takes hours to dig as deeply as he'd like, hiding and ducking out of the way every time a car approaches. He had hoped to come away with a solution, something he could write in an anonymous letter to the city government in Point Pleasant or pass on to some citizen, but no deficiency makes itself known. When he leaves that night, with sunrise dangerously near, he leaves his confidence that this will be simple behind him.

"You look tired," John says on Tuesday.

"I didn't sleep much," Indrid says.

John stays over Tuesday night and Wednesday night. He comes by Thursday after work and finds Indrid pacing sharply back and forth.

"Has something happened?" he asks carefully.

"No." Indrid doesn't mean to snap at him, but the opposite of something has happened. He's been cooped up in his house for three days now, with no plan and no sense of how to proceed. Each day that passes brings them closer to winter, closer to the fall of the bridge. He has no idea how to move forward and he's wasting time.

John crosses the room slowly and sits down at the table, eyeing Indrid like an untamed dog. Indrid makes himself stop pacing—there's no use in alienating John—but that just leaves the restless energy boiling beneath his skin with no outlet. He runs both hands roughly through his hair and tries to calm down.

"There's something on your mind." It's not a question, but Indrid nods. "Would you feel better if you shared it?"

"I can't," Indrid says.

"Why?"

And Indrid isn't sure how to respond to that.

The simplest answer is, of course, that there are rules. But he's already broken those rules. He's broken every single other rule, including the next biggest one. A more thoughtful reason is that he's not sure how John would react to this fantastical knowledge. He might laugh. He might start a witch hunt. He might sneak in and kill Indrid while he sleeps. John believes in gods and monsters, and a monster, undeniably, is what Indrid is by the standards of this planet.

"It's a long story," is what he says quietly, staring at the floor.

"Okay," John says. "That's fine. You don't have to tell me. But, Indrid?" When Indrid doesn't respond, John gets up from the table and touches his cheek until he meets his eyes. "Indrid, you *can* tell me. I promise. No matter what it is. . ." John glances away a moment. When he looks back, he's determined, but also flushed. "Indrid, I care about you. More than I've ever cared about anyone else before. I had. . . accepted, I guess, that I would be alone. That I wasn't exciting or ambitious enough to be worth anyone's time. And that fact that you're so kind and fascinating and sweet and you've found something in me to like. . . I honestly struggle to understand it, sometimes. You've let me tell you everything, let me complain and worry and let me be excited and overjoyed. I just want you to know it goes both ways. You can share this burden if you need to. No matter how bad it is, I promise it can't change the way I feel about you."

Indrid doesn't want to doubt John—it would, inevitably, hurt his feelings. But this isn't the same as whispering confessions about annoying co-workers or private dreams. This is a secret that could upend everything that Indrid's built. This is a secret that could ruin him.

"It's hard to explain," is what he says to John's soft, imploring gaze.

"I. . .I can't tell you parts of it. I can't." John frowns again and goes to move his hand away from Indrid's cheek, but he rushes to hold it in place. "I want to. But I can't, yet. But I can. . ." He thinks for a moment and then, very carefully, continues. "There's something that's going to happen. Something bad. And I know that it's going to happen. It's going to be disastrous. I might be able to stop it. But I don't know how. I can't just call a government official and explain it. I'd be locked up. And I don't know what to do. I don't know how to use this knowledge to help."

John is quiet, but this time his expression is thoughtful.

"And you can't tell me what it is?" he asks. Indrid is shaking his head before John can even finish asking. "Right. Well, I suppose, in that position . . .I would just tell people. Maybe not the authorities, but just. . .anyone who will listen."

"No one will ever believe it," Indrid says quietly.

"Sure they will. I believe it, don't I?"

"You know me."

"The very first night I met you, you told me something unbelievable," John says, once again holding Indrid's gaze. "I believed you then and I didn't know you at all. You're trustworthy and earnest and people will see that."

Indrid swallows hard against the swollen lump of shame in his throat. He's not trustworthy. He's been lying to John from the very first moment. Standing here, looking the way he is, acting the way he does, he's lying to John right now.

He licks his lips. "Not everyone is as trusting as you are," he manages to say.

"You'd be surprised," John says. He presses a soft, dry kiss to Indrid's cheek. "Give people the benefit of the doubt. They're more trusting than you'd think."

In the morning, Indrid tells John that he'll be out for the evening and agrees to meet him for lunch the next day. Once again, he watches the hours tick by, but this time, instead of waiting for the dead of night, Indrid leaves as soon as the sun has fully set. He stays lower, closer to the trees, and tries to stay far away from the lit houses and cars that he passes. The world is still awake at this hour, and he doesn't have the freedom that he's had the last few times he's flown this route.

He doesn't go straight to the bridge. Instead, he moves cautiously through the edge of town, sticking to shadows and hiding in the cover of trees. He searches the streets for people, and when he finally finds someone walking down the street on their own, he approaches cautiously, staying as hidden in the dark as he can manage.

It's a man not much older than John. Indrid perches in a tree and watches him approach, whistling.

"The Silver Bridge," Indrid calls out. His voice croaks and hisses--it's been years since he spoke in this form. The noise catches the man's attention and he whirls around. "Beware the Silver Bridge!" Indrid repeats and the man makes a choked, panicked sound. He tries to step backwards and trips, sprawling on the ground, gasping.

Indrid recognizes the fear on his face. When the man glances away to regain his footing, Indrid disappears into the trees as quickly and silently as he can manage.

That's one person told. Indrid hopes this wasn't a mistake.

He tries again and again after that.

He staggers times, days. He approaches men, women, couples. He takes John's advice and tells as many people as possible, but the ones he tells in his human form move away without engaging, ignoring him and walking in the opposite direction, and the ones he tells from the shadows in his other form panic and run. He keeps waiting for the person who will listen, the person who will recognize the urgency in his voice and ask more questions. The person who will stop this disaster before it starts.

Night after night he goes out. Night after night he dreams of the bridge. Morning after morning he reads the paper, hoping for a miracle.

It's not the bridge he finds in the paper, however. In fact, it's not even Indrid who finds it.

"Have you seen this?" John asks, amused, brandishing a newspaper over their lunch. Indrid hasn't seen anything—he's exhausted. He was out all night in Point Pleasant again and is struggling not to let it show to John, who's already been looking at him like something's wrong for days now.

"I haven't, no," Indrid says. He takes the newspaper from John and reads the headline he'd indicated. His heart drops into his stomach.

'Red-Eyed Creature' Reported in W. Va, the paper says.

Indrid thinks he may be sick.

"A monster," John says, grinning. "People will believe anything these days."

Indrid barely hears him, skimming the article. It says nothing about his message or warning—the report was given by a couple who spotted him while in their car. He had hoped that if people were going to see him, report on him, they'd at least mention the bridge, but. . .

"Indrid?" John's fingers press against his inner wrist where it's lying on the table. "Is something wrong?"

So much is wrong.

"No," he murmurs. He forces himself to hand the paper back to John. "I'm sorry, I'm very tired."

"I've noticed," John says. He's still frowning, still pressing his fingers against the delicate skin of Indrid's wrist, this fragile part of his human-like body. "I know you've had something on your mind. I know you felt you couldn't tell me before. Has anything changed?"

Maybe this is a good segue. Maybe this is the best opportunity that Indrid will ever have to tell John what he is and what he's doing.

Or maybe John will think he's a monster, the same as the humans in the car.

"I'm sorry," he whispers, looking away from John and down at the table. "It hasn't. I can't."

"That's okay," John says, and he sounds like he means it, but Indrid wonders how long that will last.

Indrid's dreams have become more detailed. He hears the screaming in a constant roar, now, the screeching of metal on metal, the splintering of wood. He can see individual cars, can see people inside of them scrambling to get out. He can see the twisted metal sinking to the bottom of the river.

He wakes after each of them, shaking. Sometimes John is there to hold him steady and sometimes he's alone. On the nights he's alone, if it's not too close to morning, he flies out to Point Pleasant and looks for anyone, *anyone* walking the streets. He's told dozens of people now, warned dozens of people, but winter is coming and there's been nothing in the papers about the bridge. He wrote a letter to the paper, even, sent it anonymously, begging a reporter to look into the state of the bridge.

Nothing. There's been nothing. And time is running out.

He knows time is short when he wakes up from the dream clawing at his ears and screaming.

"Indrid!" John is shaking him and it takes Indrid too long to understand that he's not under the icy Ohio River, but tangled in his sheets. He's not drowning, the dampness on his face is only tears and blood. "For god's sake, Indrid! Wake up!"

John slaps him and Indrid gasps and rolls out of the bed and onto the floor, dazed and breathing hard.

Indrid has had more dreams of the future than he can count. They've been a part of his life since his youth. Not a single one has ever upset him like this. There hasn't ever been a single dream that's made him weep the way this one has. He's losing his mind.

John is kneeling next to him on the floor, rubbing his back and murmuring apologies.

"I didn't know what to do. I'm so sorry, darling, I didn't know what else to do. Are you okay? Please be okay, Indrid."

"I'm fine," Indrid manages to say, even though his voice wobbles and breaks on the second word. "I'm just. . .a dream. I'm sorry."

John hugs him, hard, trembling a little himself. Indrid lowers his head and lets himself inhale the scent of John's hair.

"You scared me," John mumbles. "God, you scared me."

They sit like that for long minutes until they're both finally calm. John's eyes are red and wet when he draws himself back. Indrid's sure his own aren't much better.

"You've scratched yourself," John whispers, touching the side of Indrid's face just below his ear. Indrid tries not to flinch, but it stings. "Indrid, please. God, please just tell me. Just tell me what's going on. I'm worried about you."

"I know," Indrid says. He closes his eyes again. "I wish I could."

John helps Indrid to his feet and makes him sit on the edge of the bed. He wets a rag in the kitchen and then comes back and gently washes the blood off of Indrid's face, then sits down next to him.

"You can trust me," John says softly.

Indrid very badly wants to believe it, but he stays silent all the same.

They sleep poorly for the rest of the night and John leaves for work in the morning with a promise to return. Indrid is distracted and distant and laser focused on the time. He gained one terrible thing from the latest dream, and that was the time on the clock in one of the ill-fated cars as it plunged into the freezing water.

He has less than twelve hours left to stop the disaster that's nearly upon them.

He can't fly to Point Pleasant in the daytime, not the way he can at night. Instead, he hitches a ride up the road as far as he can go and walks the last leg of the trip. He doesn't know what he's going to do once he gets to Point Pleasant; all the begging and warning of the past two months has yielded nothing and there's no reason to believe it will start now.

He walks through the town, marveling at how different it looks in the sunlight. How peaceful. It's after lunch and the winter streets are largely empty. Indrid, always conspicuous to begin with, is out of place in his large black coat as he lingers on the sidewalks, staring into storefronts and hoping he won't recognize anyone inside from his dreams.

He stops and buys a cup of coffee.

"Don't cross the bridge tonight," he murmurs to the girl at the cash register. She smiles absently, barely paying attention.

"Stay away from the bridge," he tells a couple standing outside the general store, comparing lists. They nod politely at him without looking up.

"Beware the Silver Bridge!" he hisses insistently at a man crossing to the bank. He rolls his eyes and goes out of his way to avoid Indrid on the sidewalk.

He does that all afternoon.

It's utterly useless.

In the end, he retreats to the abandoned munitions factory as the sun sets.

He doesn't know what else to do.

He should be able to stop this, but he doesn't know what else to do.

He sits on the roof and stares at the river.

When the bridge begins to fall, he doesn't let himself look away.

Indrid flees once the bridge goes down. It's cowardly, maybe, but it's not as if there's anything he can do to help in the aftermath. He tried to stop it and he failed and the cries of the dying already haunt his dreams. There's no reason to linger.

He flies for a time and then, terrified that he'll be found out, he takes his human form and he walks.

It's very cold.

When he's too tired to walk any further, he makes his way through the woods to the road and sticks out his thumb. A man in a pick-up truck eventually slows to a stop and gestures for him to get in the passenger size.

"Where you going?" he asks.

"Parkersburg," Indrid croaks.

"Good choice," the man says. "You don't wanna be heading back that way. The whole damn bridge collapsed in Point Pleasant."

Indrid doesn't reply. He's afraid if he opens his mouth, he'll scream.

The man drives him back towards home in silence.

All Indrid wants to do is sleep. All he wants to do is scream and break something. All he wants to do is cry.

All these rules, all these edicts he's used to live his life and what use were they once he was alone? And then he rids himself of them and has a chance to really do something, really give something back to this planet that's sustaining him, and he can't manage that either.

What is the point of these premonitions? Why does he have them if he's not meant to stop these things? What has he done that the universe has chosen to torture him like this?

The light is on in his house when he trudges through the woods and to his front door.

He doesn't need a vision to know that John is waiting for him inside.

He tries, fruitlessly, to wipe the tears from his eyes as he enters the cabin.

"You're okay," is the first thing John says, his entire body sagging with relief.

"I am," Indrid says carefully. John is sitting at his table. There is a stack of bridge drawings in front of him.

"You've been gone all day."

"I have," Indrid says. He doesn't move any further into the room.

"The Silver Bridge collapsed this evening," he says. "I heard about it on the radio."

Indrid doesn't respond.

"It's the bridge you've been drawing."

Indrid doesn't respond to that, either.

"Indrid, you need to tell me what to think here, because. . . I don't like the things my mind is trying to conclude." He stares at Indrid, half worried, half resolute. When Indrid says nothing, something in John breaks. There are tears in his eyes. "Indrid, please. *Please*. You've been different for weeks. For months. Something's been on your mind. It's been hurting you. I swear you can confide in me." Indrid swallows against the lump in his throat. John blinks back tears. "Indrid," he whispers, "*I love you*. I promise. Just. Please."

The world tilts beneath Indrid's feet. He's so *tired*.

"John. . . " Indrid says hoarsely.

"Please." John gets to his feet and walks slowly towards Indrid, then takes his hands. "Please, Indrid."

Indrid closes his eyes. "I have nothing else in this world besides you," he says. "If I tell you, I'll lose you. I'll be alone."

"You *won't*," John insists. He sounds so fierce that Indrid almost believes him.

Indrid opens his eyes. He leads John over to the table and sits in one of the chairs. John, slowly, sits in the other.

"You will not believe what I am about to say," Indrid says. He hasn't seen this in a vision, but he's not stupid. "You will not believe what I am about to say and you will get angry or scared or you will think I'm crazy. You will not react well. And then you will leave. Do you understand that?"

"You don't get to make those decisions for me," John says, but he sounds as tired as Indrid feels.

Indrid closes his eyes again. He remembers long nights and bright mornings with John here in this little house. He remembers talking for hours and hours. He remembers the way that John smiles at him sometimes, like he's all that matters in the world.

He wants so desperately to believe that John truly loves him. He wants so desperately to believe that John will still be here tomorrow.

"My family does not originate on this planet," Indrid says, looking John straight in the eye. "We are not of this earth. We have been here for many years. We have certain abilities, among them, the ability to see visions of the future. Premonitions."

Lines of confusion are slowly furrowing John's brow.

"For months now, I've seen the Silver Bridge collapsing," Indrid continues. "I've seen many things, but that one has returned over and over again. The first rule of our society has always been that we don't interfere, but I'm the only one left, now. I'm the last of my kind, and I wanted to help." Unexpectedly, his throat gets slick and tight. "I just wanted to help. I wanted to *help*." He squeezes his eyes shut and then wipes at them roughly with the back of his hand. When he opens them again, John has gone pale. "I couldn't help. I couldn't change anything. The bridge is gone."

"You don't—this is—you're right, I do think you're—" John's face won't land on one expression, cycling back and forth between half a dozen, too quickly for Indrid to track. "You're—you're not, Indrid, what are you—"

The one consistent part of his expression, though, is the hardness. The soft edges of his John are gone. The light in his eyes is out.

Indrid feels the light go out in his own. He should stop now. He should walk this back. He should lie and pretend it's all a terrible joke.

You'd be surprised, John had said of humanity's ability to trust. *Give people the benefit of the doubt.*

If anyone has earned it, it's John.

Indrid stands up. He looks at John. He wishes he had thought to memorize his face long ago when he was happy or laughing or sleeping against Indrid's chest. Instead, he's confused and furious as Indrid studies him for a moment before taking a deep breath and shifting forms.

The silence in the cabin is deafening.

It lasts five seconds before John chokes on a scream and falls backwards against the floor.

Indrid shifts back immediately, moves around the table to kneel next to John.

"I'm no different than I was, John," Indrid insists, but when he reaches out to help John up, he throws himself in the other direction.

"Stay away from me!" John shouts. "What—what *are* you?"

"I'm me," Indrid says softly. "I'm the same person I've always been. John, I swear—"

John's on his feet, finally, grabbing for his coat and stumbling towards the door.

"You're a monster!" John shouts.

Indrid takes a ragged, pained breath. "I love you," he whispers.

"You're *not him*," John hisses back, and then he's gone, running away and into the night.

It takes Indrid ten minutes to pack what he needs, but only after he spends ten minutes ridding himself of the heaving, guttural sobs that leave him immobile on the floor.

He sets the pile of drawings on the table on fire and waits until the table catches before walking out into the night.

He takes to the sky while his little house full of his soft, comfortable things burns behind him.

He doesn't look back.

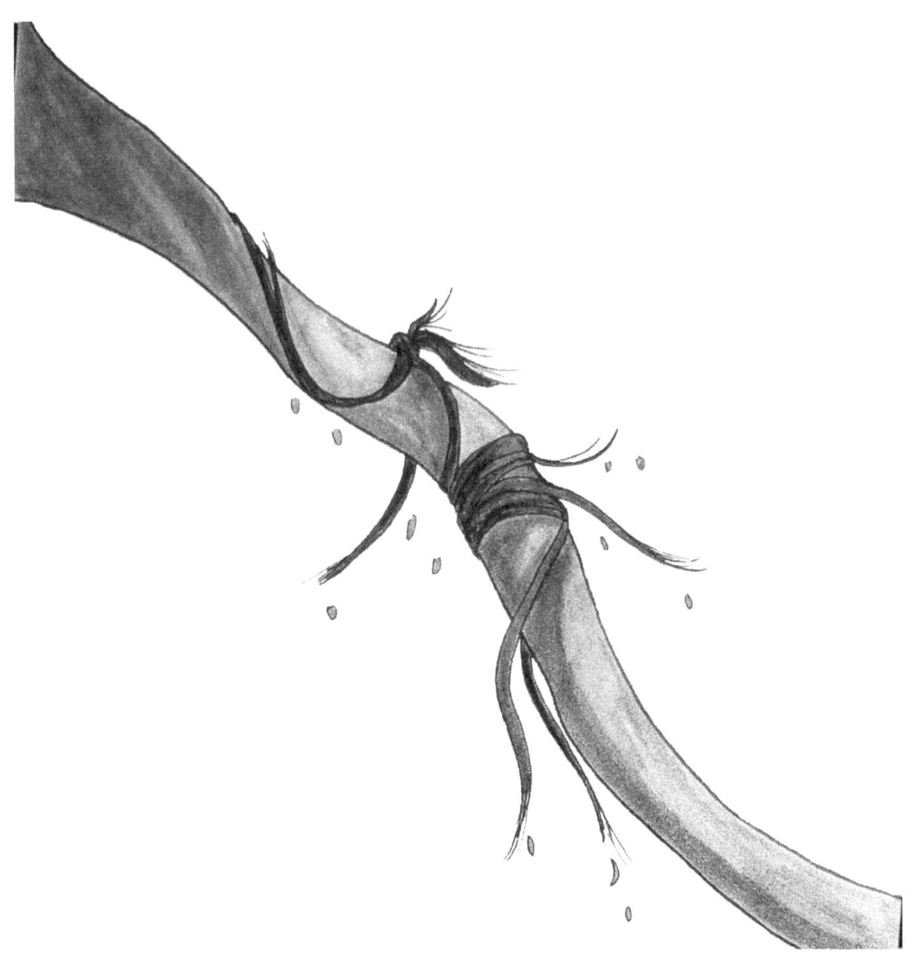

That Which Should Become

Christine Ricketts

It is the tree that captures all your attention and focus. There is simply nowhere else to look, no space that is not occupied by the massive trunk or the thick branches that stretch out in every direction. There are as many spiraling limbs as there are stars, perhaps even more; the brown-grey tendrils block out swatches of the sky with their span. Even though it is midday and the sun is high overhead, the base of the tree is shrouded. All around, hanging from every branch like long, dangling fingers are lengths of twisted twine, some soaked dark with water, still dripping, and others faded pale and stiff, dry near as bone.

If the branches of the tree reach out like a never-ending expanse of arms, then along the ground just as many roots bump up like legs kicking free of the earth. Some rise up high to form arches before plunging back down into the soil—giant worms burrowing passage to other realms.

When at last your eyes grow accustomed to the sight, no longer over-whelmed by the sheer volume and spread of the tree, you can see the forms shifting within the shade. It takes a moment to recognize the three distinct shapes, moving with a mixture of fluid grace, deliberation, and slow rigidity. The roots are obstacles and aids that the figures avoid and use in equal measure.

In the center, built in front of the tree like an offering out of rough grey stone, is a well. Three women move about it with varying degrees of ease—two stand upright and walk unimpeded. The third hunches and hobbles, as twisted as the twine that blows in the breeze.

You aren't sure why you are there but the longer you stand and stare, the more you begin to suspect.

You've seen them only once before—a brief memory that seems impossible for you to have. The day of your birth, when you first came crying into the world, the bright white light giving way to speckled color. They were there, all three, like a painting stepped forward from off a wall. They said nothing, spoke to no one, simply remained as silent witnesses marking the occasion.

Much as you stand now, just beyond the roots of the great tree. You haven't made a sound, you know that, for years of living with four siblings has made you quiet as a mouse. And still the third woman, old, seemingly blind unopened eyes, and probably deaf, has somehow become aware of you. She beckons you forward and nothing you think convinces your feet to stay still.

"Come, take the thread here," she croons, her voice still bold and clear despite her fragile form.

"Mind the roots," she warns as you scramble through them, awkward and unbalanced, to where she is perched. She holds the dark material out to you—it lies across the crooked joints of her fingers like frayed fishing net.

You touch the strands with your own trembling fingers that feel blunt and clumsy as they try and gather the threads. They feel somehow sticky and slippery at the same time and as you pull your hand back, one of the threads falls loose and drifts toward the ground.

It is snatched from the air by those knobby digits and slipped back into the gathering in your hand.

"Careful. Time is tricky to keep hold of," she admonishes with a toothless smile. You curl your fingers around the threads   .

"What—" you swallow as she looks at you, eyelids closed so that you wonder if there is anything behind the thin skin. "What am I to do with it?"

The crone rests her fingers together.

"You will twine it. Not too loose and not too tight."

"How—" You swallow again. "How do I *know*?"

Another smile. "No one knows."

You don't understand and yet, slowly, you begin to twist and roll the strings, trying to imagine it is simply wool that you are spinning, even if it is nothing like the wool from your father's farm. Nothing like it at all. You cast your eyes about and frown—you cannot tell from where the threads are pulling. There are no bags or piles—only the tree, the roots, the well and the women.

"How long do I . . ." you trail off, fingers still twisting, the movement familiar even if the material is not.

"Spin until it becomes what it should."

Your frown deepens. "But how do I—"

Before you can finish a figure cuts in front of you and takes hold of the string you've just begun to weave together. Your head falls back in order to see—she rises so much higher than either you or the crone. Pale blond hair is braided tightly to her head, like a crown that you can barely see, given how far away it is. She nods without speaking to you and frees the thread with the flick of a black bladed dagger.

Then she pushes away, keeping your attention as she steps to the well. Without hesitation she kneels, dips the twine into the water and then rises, raising it overhead. The short string glistens, dark and wet, though not a drop of water beads on the line. It flutters as she ties it neatly to a branch, an erratic movement made without the breath of wind behind it.

You're mesmerized by the sight of it, swaying ever so slightly. And even as you watch, seconds ticking by, the thread lightens, back towards the weathered grey it began as. No sooner has it been strung up is it taken down by a third set of hands. Strong, with long straight fingers, thicker than your own. Deftly, they undo the knot with a quick tug and then cradle the string down to the roots that erupt from the ground. The hands lay the thread flat, the grey pale against the earth stained wood.

With a gentle press, the twine sinks, swallowed into the flesh of the tree.

You look back to the crone but she has shuffled away to the well and there is more thread to twine. You begin again, your fingers steady as you watch her slow progress over the great roots.

The tall woman takes a cup from the well and pours water over the roots where the old crone kneels. The second woman, with such firm hands, pulls a long-parched thread from one of the highest branches.

Your fingers pull and twist without the aid of your eyes.

Around the crone the thread is wrapped, carefully as a wedding shawl and veil. With hands unbent or crooked, they press at the crone's shoulders, gently, gently.

You watch, still twisting, still twining.

The crone sinks slowly into the roots, wrinkled and gnarled, quiet and steady, like the tree above and below.

Twist. Pull. Twist. Pull.

The old woman is gone. The thread is pulled from your fingers, taken to the well, tied to the branches.

You reach for the next.

Hydrophilia

Nicole DeGennaro

Letha crawls up the beach sputtering, choking on water and air alike. The waves crash over her, but instead of trying to pull her back they nudge her forward. Inch by inch, until she's past the breakers and the sea can barely reach to caress her ankles. She stays on her side, coughing up liquid until finally she can suck in one breath, then another, without struggling.

Her dark, sopping hair clings to her face. She rolls onto her back. The sky hangs gray above her, mirroring the sea's mood. She knew better than to try swimming in this weather, but something about the tumultuous waves had called to her, matching her own nebulous restlessness. It wouldn't be ignored.

Despite nearly drowning, it's like the saltwater has replaced the blood in her veins. Everything feels more immediate, every emotion larger than one person can contain. Her discontent hasn't been washed away, but it has found a rhythm to match the ocean, and it soothes her.

She drags herself to her feet and turns back to the water, watching it make its slow retreat with each wave. When she closes her eyes, she can almost hear a whisper from the sea, getting fainter and fainter.

Go, go.

A thunderclap startles her as the clouds above burst, but she hardly notices the rain; she's already soaked. As if in defiance, she takes a few steps toward the water, a part of her longing to leap back in and follow its currents as far as she can. Instead, she forces herself to take one step back, then another, until all she can do to keep her heart from breaking is to turn away, hunch her shoulders against the rain, and go.

The next time Letha sees the sea, something has changed.

She is crying in inexplicable happiness, which on its own isn't alarming.

As she stands watching light refract on the surface of the lazy waves, she traces the source of the feeling back in her mind to a vivid memory of a child graduating college, the first in her family to do so. Her happiness is a parent's pride as that child walks across the stage to collect her diploma.

But Letha has no children.

She came to the water to calm the storm brewing within her. This isn't the first time she's recalled something that she never experienced. At first, she wanted to write it off as a vivid imagination, or maybe even a glimpse of a past life. But all these unconnected fragments linger; she can reach for them again and again, and the emotion never dulls. Each of them is jagged at both ends, a piece of a full picture she's never seen. They're nothing more than detritus floating within her.

After it happened once, it kept happening, as if the first time had been a catalyst for a process she could not control. And these discarded moments were everywhere, shells on a beach for the taking. With the initial one she was fascinated, wanted to feel the shape of it, admire its form. She didn't know she wouldn't be able to put it back. After that, the shells became barnacles, seeking her out, clinging to her mind, multiplying. Crowding her out of herself. One day it would be a momentary sadness no longer needed; the next, a desperate longing for something that had finally been obtained; then, the anger from a misunderstanding long settled.

All these and more come to Letha, a thousand pieces from lives she never lived. She supposes people have to shed these moments to make room for new ones. What she doesn't understand is why she has to collect them.

So, she goes to the sea for answers, not knowing what else to do when a panic—all her own—begins to overtake her. It is a brilliantly sunny day, and though there are others enjoying the weather and the water, they pay her as little attention as she pays them. Once she reaches the wet sand, she slips off her shoes and socks and carries them as she walks into the shallow water.

The waves trip over one another to greet her, and soon the sea is already an inch over her ankles, going on two. The effect on her is instantaneous; it is as if the water is flowing through her, cleansing and soothing. She smiles and closes her eyes. Once again, the sea whispers to her.

Full, full.

Somewhere the pressure of all those fragments is being released. She is so overwhelmed by the relief that it takes her longer than it should to realize the water is spiriting away all the foreign memories she has collected, leaving her lighter, unburdened. Tears flow freely down her cheeks, racing to join the saltwater engulfing her up to her knees now. She isn't sure if she moved further in or if that much time has passed.

Before she can figure it out, the waves are receding. The urge to follow tugs at her, but she is distracted by something the sea left behind. At first, she thinks it is a memory it forgot to collect, but the shape of this one is familiar, a fragment of a picture she does know. The water has gifted her something precious. But it is small, and although it is recognizable, she doesn't have the context to make sense of it.

All she learns from it is that it is the ocean's purpose to remember. And it is her purpose to forget.

Knowing her purpose doesn't make it easier. She still spends every day living pieces of other people's lives. She has experienced more triumphs and failures than one person could fathom, and yet none of them are hers to claim.

With each sunset she misses the sea more and more. She spends most of her time at the beach because she has nowhere else to go. And whenever she brings it things to remember, things for her to forget, the water gives her a piece of herself back as a reward.

Or, it seemed like a reward at first. But each piece only helps create the outline of herself, not the substance. She is left empty, not restored, so she can continue to collect what the water craves. Now that she knows the shape of herself, her desperation is worse, because she has become aware of how much is still missing. She could spend her entire life ferrying these fragments from the land to the sea and never retrieve enough of herself to make it worthwhile.

"I can't," she tells the water. "I can't do it anymore." She closes her eyes, expecting the waves to whisper encouragement. Instead, they say nothing.

How long has she been doing this? It's easy to lose track of time when your experiences are an amalgamation of everyone else's and your own memories are lost at sea. All she knows is that it has become impossible for her to leave the beach. She has somehow become more like the water and less like a human. It is intolerable.

"Say something!" she demands, alone with the water under the night sky, its surface a dark mirror. She wades into the waves, up to her waist, feels the pull of the undertow and how the rhythm of her blood changes to match the current. Desperate, she reaches into the depths with her hands, waiting to be noticed.

This time, though, she hasn't brought it anything but herself. Something unidentifiable has filled up all the space within her and is spilling over her edges. She can't name it because if she has felt it before, she doesn't have the memory. But it hurts.

The water creeps up as the tide comes in. Letha doesn't relent, even though she knows nothing is as patient as the sea. The moon floats across the darkness, and the silence carries on. Letha starts to cry and looks up at the stars. The waves reach her chest. And that is when, finally, the water calls her home.

Come, come.

The current pulls her under with a gentle tug. She doesn't bother taking one last gasp of air, instead opening her lungs to the water. The human part of her panics, thrashing and trying to find the surface again. The liquid part of her rejoices.

And then, there's no longer a distinction between the two.

The currents are all new and yet familiar. She spends time exploring them, relearning and remembering. The journey brings her down deep, until it's only her and creatures not yet seen by human eyes. She realizes the water is leading her to its greatest treasure trove, the only collection for which it is willing to share custody: Letha's own memories. Not the ones she's gathered from above, but the ones that are all hers. The ones that will make her whole.

The ocean understands her history is too valuable to be scattered in its infinite depths like everything else, so it keeps her memories safe for her until she returns. Still, it is reluctant to part with them. After leading Letha into its most coveted grotto, the water makes her wait. But now that she is mostly liquid again, Letha has a greater well of patience, and there is nothing more worth her time than herself.

While waiting, she swirls between the detritus in the depths, recognizing them as fragments she has saved from oblivion. The most unique and precious ones find their way here, like she did, where they are slowly buried in silt to keep them safe. Now that they are not weighing Letha down, she has a greater appreciation for them. Even in the darkness they shimmer like so many bioluminescent fish.

And the collection goes back, back beyond human memory. Water is a metaphor for time because both came into being so close together that they are in many ways indistinguishable. The depths preserve that history, covering species humans have not yet found fossils of, moments that no one recalls but the ocean. Water, like time, has a reputation for wiping things away, but few consider what happens to those things once they are taken. They are not obliterated; they are preserved.

A motion catches her attention; a vessel like a long, slender boat emerges from the shadows, bobbing along the currents toward her. It summons a sense of familiarity, but when she reaches for the memory there is a gap. It is one that the vessel contains.

The ocean delivers it to Letha, and she cradles it for a moment as if she is greeting a lost child. The boat is full to the brim, holding more than seems possible for its size. But she doesn't hesitate to pull out the stopper, and the contents surge out, carrying her away in a rush. As she spins end over end into the deep, a watery voice whispers to her.

Home, home.

She lets the ocean carry her where it will while she is reacquainted with herself. At first the part of her that is still human struggles to understand the chronology of her existence, although the fluid part of her grasps it immediately: there is none. It all has happened and is happening and will happen. In her own way, she too is a collection.

This understanding hones her awareness of her boundaries; even though she and the ocean are both liquids, she is a different density, still somewhat separate. Creatures weave between her and the sea without realizing they are crossing any border, but it is there. Irrelevant to anything but her.

Letha isn't sure how long this liminal period lasts; her attention is entirely on learning her history, her present, her future. Every living creature sheds intangible things; perhaps not memories per se, but even a cell carries some recollection of its existence. Its parts know their purpose, and when they cease to function, she collects that knowledge. This is what she has always done and will always do.

So, when everything lived in the sea, she too resided solely in the water. When the first creature grew legs and crawled ashore, the waves tried to reach up after it. But the distance was too great, so Letha was sent into the air, to fall as rain and collect what she could as she meandered home. And when the creatures were small and short-lived, that strategy sufficed. But as humans came to be, from primitive to modern, the sea had to evolve as well. Instead of being ferried by rivers, she for a time became a river, and a ferry sailed upon her. It's the same long, slender boat that now keeps her memories safe.

Eventually, even that form became obsolete. The sea hungered for more, and fewer and fewer people were sent along her currents. So, it called her home; by this point it knew enough to remake her into something new: not quite water, and not quite human. A being that could move between the two.

The first time, she was sent ashore during a tempest, one that swept away houses and transformed the landscape. The sea feared it had not made her human enough, that she would suffocate in the air and be unable to return home. But when the sky cleared, when all the rainwater evaporated, she remained. Intact. Empty. Alone.

Most of these memories play out the same: she survives for a time ashore, carrying her collected burden to the sea to empty herself and do it again and again until her longing for the water finally turns into a desperation that drives her home. At first, she is captivated by each instance, how sometimes she goes decades before she walks into the water and other times, she barely lasts a few months.

For a time, she enjoys having her full self back. She lets the moon carry her across the world, lets the arctic chill her and the Mediterranean warm her. But as she knows better than anyone, everything has a weight. And when you have existed as long as Letha, it becomes too much to carry.

She never expected that a sense of longing would still haunt her after she reacquired her own memories. But the feeling tails her like a predator, lurking where light doesn't penetrate. It's the realization that humans aren't the only ones who have an emptiness they cannot fill.

As if sensing her rising dread, the sea tries to soothe her.

Stay, stay.

There are more revelations hiding in her memories than she anticipated, and no matter how hard she tries she cannot outswim them. While technically she cannot drown, she begins to suffocate all the same.

Her life is an inescapable cycle. She believed she had returned home, but she has no home. The longer she is in the sea, the more she pines for land. She is not part water and part human; she is Letha. It is the whole of her that yearns, not one aspect over another.

As existence evolves, so does she. It cannot be undone, so she must live with it. And the only way she can is to forget. The comfort of that thought is a ballast against her panic. But it doesn't make breathing any easier. Knowing how to reset the cycle doesn't make it more bearable. If she has no choice about whether to participate in the process, she is at least grateful to have control over when the ending becomes the beginning.

She is not the only one grappling with cycles. Now that she knows her own, she spots them everywhere. The way the atmosphere snatches water from the sea and rains it over distant lands, only for it to eventually find its way back to the ocean to be evaporated once again. The way a creature lives and then dies, and in its decay causes other things to spring to life.

The way everything forgets, remembers, and then forgets again. It looks different on the outside, but the underlying processes are the same. This is the final realization Letha makes: she thought her uniqueness was the painful part, but it's not. It's the fact that she's the only one with any control. This knowledge makes her purpose easier but her existence harder.

Everything else is only aware of its life in a line, because there comes a point where what's been forgotten is irretrievable. The sea harbors those memories, but they cannot be extracted. Letha is the only thing that keeps them from being entirely lost. Most of the preserved memories seem similar at first glance, but because Letha has contained them all she knows that each one is special in some way. Each one is worthy of being collected by the sea.

She smiles to herself as, for the first time since regaining her own memories, she understands. All her previous revelations were true in their own way, but now they've coalesced. She comes from the sea to forget, and she comes to the sea to remember. Her purpose is a burden, but it is also a gift. As are most things. Humans need to forget to make space for something new, but when you are as infinite as time itself, you need not make such concessions. Without her, all of these precious experiences would be entirely lost.

Letha makes her way toward the surface; she had sunk so far into the depths during her despair that it is a while before she sees a glimmer of sunlight dancing on the water. The vessel surges up from the darkness to follow her, ready to collect what she must discard.

As she rises to meet the light, the sea speaks to her.

Leave, leave.

Letha tumbles in the waves, and when she hits the beach the impact knocks the wind from her lungs. Still submerged, she fights the impulse to breathe in and instead flails until one of her arms finds the surface. She kicks her legs and breaks through the water, immediately sucking in air. Now that she knows which way is up, she can get her feet under her and make her way to the shore.

The waves seem to calm as her pulse does, slowing and shrinking until the sea is almost unnaturally still around her. She hesitates as she reaches the edge of the water, the foam clinging to her feet. Something about it calls to her; for a brief moment, she considers diving back in.

But when she looks up at the beach, glittering in the sun, it also calls to her. The water will always be there, but for now the pull of the shore is stronger. Letha takes one step forward, then another. As she moves out of the sea's reach onto the drying sand, a faint voice whispers to her, coming from nowhere but speaking directly to her heart.

Go, go.

PART IV

Urban Legend
a humorous or horrific story or piece of information circulated as though true, especially one purporting to involve someone vaguely related or known to the teller.

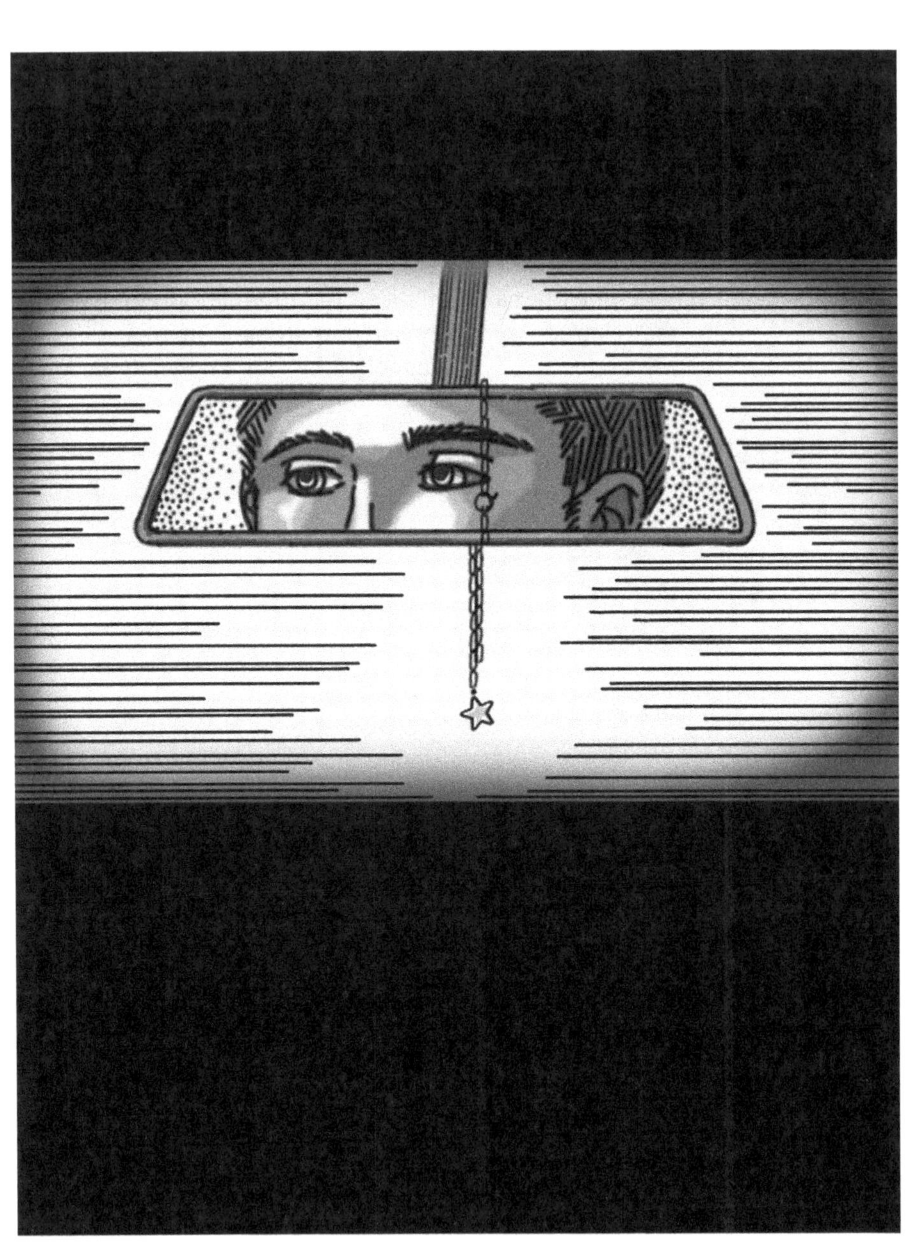

THE HITCHHIKER

KAITLYN SUDOL

The problem is, no one stops for hitchhikers these days.

Eddy understands why. Danger has increased. Technology has evolved. People think anyone who would hitchhike is crazy, ergo, they're quick to avoid letting said crazy person into their car.

The moon hangs above her, a big, bulbous, orange orb. She sticks out her thumb and keeps walking.

Once, in the nineties, two guys stopped their beat-up minivan. It was like something out of a cautionary tale, but Eddy got in. The guys were nice, as it turned out. High as fuck, but normal. Ethan and Jason, their names were.

She wonders, sometimes, what happened to them.

Eddy met Teresa at church camp, of all places. Teresa's skirts were always an appropriate length and she had white sneakers that were somehow always clean. She wore light pink lipstick. Eddy hated her for a full day before she walked in on her slipping a flask out from her suitcase with a beleaguered sigh. That afternoon, they became friends.

A week later, they became friends with certain benefits.

A week after that, Eddy was in love.

This evening, another minivan stops. It's a mom.

(They're always moms.)

"I normally wouldn't stop," she says through the crack of an inched-down passenger window, "but you look so cold."

She looks like somebody's daughter is what the woman means. Eddy's been at this long enough to be fluent in the language.

"I sure do appreciate it," she says, and gets into the back. Sure enough, there's an empty car seat strapped into the middle seat and the floor is covered with Cheerios.

"Sorry about the mess," the woman says, looking cautiously at Eddy in the rearview mirror.

"I don't mind at all," Eddy says, and the woman uses her blinker to merge back onto the empty highway.

Eddy's mother didn't care about Teresa. Eddy's mother didn't care about a lot of things.

"I'm busy, Edwina," was her mantra, punctuated by a long sigh. Eddy's mother was tired most days, juggling three jobs to keep the lights on. Sometimes the lights still went off for a little while, but never for all that long, and it wasn't like the two of them were home often enough to miss them. Eddy's mother was always at work, Eddy was always at work or school, and the few moments she had to herself were reserved for Teresa.

And that, really, was the only thing about Teresa that her mother objected to.

"Do you think we can afford the gas to send you lollygagging back and forth between here and California?" her mother would snap. "Really, Edwina, show some sense! If you want to drive around so badly you can get your own car!"

That was a joke, really—Eddy didn't make nearly enough to afford a car reliable enough to put that many miles on it that regularly. She considered, for a moment, whether she had anything worth selling, but if she could have afforded anything nice enough to finance a car, she probably wouldn't be in that position in the first place. The nicest thing she owned was a necklace passed down from her grandmother, a gold star given to Eddy by her mother in a fit of sentimentality not long after the funeral. She liked her grandmother too much to think about parting with it.

So, it became her Saturday afternoon ritual: get off work, change her clothes, pack a bag, and head out to the highway with her thumb stuck out, hoping someone driving through their sleepy Nevada town was headed to California.

She takes things, sometimes.

Nothing big, of course. She doesn't think of it as *stealing*. It's a tiny memento to remember the ride, something to take with her when she leaves.

A sweater. A pair of gloves. A water bottle. From the mother in the minivan, she takes a tiny stuffed pig.

She doesn't keep them—she couldn't, even if she wanted to. She makes sure they get back to their owners. It's just nice to have something, sometimes. Just for a little while. It's nice to pretend she could have nice things if she wanted them.

Teresa didn't like the hitchhiking.

"You could take my car," she offered one day, fiddling with the latest in a line of delicate gold crosses she wore around her neck, yet another gift from her absentee father. Eddy tried not to roll her eyes as she took a long drag off the cigarette they were sharing.

Teresa's house wasn't the sort of place where the power got turned off.

"I can't take your car," Eddy said. "My mother would have a fit. Besides, what would your parents say?"

Teresa gnawed on her lower lip. It should have been attractive, but the worry knitted across her brow just made it infantilizing.

"It's fine," Eddy insisted, waving the whole conversation away. "I'm here, aren't I? And your parents aren't."

"They aren't," Teresa agreed, and relaxed a little, taking the cigarette back from Eddy. "We should take advantage of that."

It's raining. For a desert, it sure seems to Eddy like it rains a lot around here. She pulls her hood down farther over her face and keeps walking.

She's drenched by the time a car finally stops, rolling slowly along the shoulder and then backing up to where she's standing in a rapidly forming puddle. It's a sedan—nothing flashy—and a man in his thirties peers out the rolled down window at her.

"You look like you need a lift," he says with a smile she's sure he means to be charming.

What was your first clue? she doesn't say. She forces a smile and nods instead. She's been waiting for a long time, now. She can't risk scaring him off.

She gets in the car. It's dark and the street lamps are few and far between, but the dome light is just bright enough for her to take in his face, his greying hair, and the delicate gold star hanging on a necklace from his rearview mirror before the door closes and they're both bathed in darkness.

There was a boy from Teresa's youth group who was a menace from the start. Matthew. He followed Teresa all over camp and, Eddy was dismayed to learn, followed her all over the neighborhood back home, too.

"He's harmless," Teresa would insist after spending too many minutes politely declining his advances and trying to convince him to go back home. Eddy's time with Teresa was limited on their weekends together—she didn't want to waste it watching Teresa trying to convince Matthew to leave them alone.

"He's creepy," Eddy said. "He's obsessed with you."

"He's obsessed with every girl who's nice to him."

"Then be less nice to him."

Teresa rolled her eyes and flopped back onto her bed. Eddy followed suit.

"He doesn't like me," Eddy said.

"It's not that he doesn't like you," Teresa said, "he's just intimidated by you. He's not used to girls like you." Eddy snorted. "Anyway, why are we still talking about Matthew? You didn't hitch all the way here to talk about Matthew."

Eddy also didn't hitch all the way to Teresa's to listen to her entertain Matthew for an hour before politely shoving him out, but instead of pointing that out, she kissed Teresa.

Teresa kissed her back, and neither of them thought about Matthew for the rest of the day.

"So," the man says as Eddy settles into the backseat, "what's your name?"

"Elizabeth," Eddy says. She's not stupid.

"Pretty name," he says. "Terrible night to be out."

"Mmhmm," she says, as if she's not out every night, as if she has a choice.

"Going anywhere in particular?"

"East," she says. "Into Nevada. Just to the next rest stop is fine."

"Anything to help," he says, and gives her a smile that's almost sincere as he pulls back onto the road.

It took Matthew nearly six months of snooping to jump to the conclusion that Eddy's mom made after hearing about Teresa for a total of five minutes. Eddy had to give him credit—she honestly thought it would take him much longer.

He was waiting for her on Saturday, pacing around the top of Teresa's street when Eddy turned the corner.

"You!" he whispered, though there was no one else to hear. Eddy pointed at herself slowly, which ruffled him. He took an involuntary step backward, then two rapid steps forward, as if to hide his hesitation. "You're here! Again! And I know why!"

Eddy rolled her eyes and walked past him.

"I do!" he insisted. She kept walking. "I know you and Teresa are . . .are . . .doing *ungodly things*!"

He hissed the end of the sentence and Eddy had to bite back laughter.

"Fuck off, kid," she said, and kept walking.

"You're *tainting her*!" he hissed again, running after her. She easily outpaced him and he had to jog to keep up with her steady stride. "You're. . .tempting her and ruining her! You're making her sin!"

"No one makes Teresa do anything she doesn't want to do," Eddy said, which was a more PG version of the comment she wanted to make about how frequently it was Teresa tearing her clothes off and putting her hand underneath Eddy's blouse nearly before they were finished saying hello.

"You don't even feel bad about it!" Matthew continued.

"You're right," Eddy said. "I don't." She sped up—it was evolving from funny to annoying. She just wanted to see Teresa, not bother with his asshole. He started running after her, but she picked up her pace and sprinted the last two houses until she was in Teresa's front door with the lock turned firmly behind her. Teresa glanced up, both pleased and confused.

"I'm not done with you!" Matthew yelled from the other side of the door. Eddy flipped the door off and sighed, throwing her hair over her shoulder and shrugging at Teresa.

"Hey."

Teresa stared over her shoulder at the door.

"Seriously, T, ignore him," Eddy said.

But she should have known that wasn't the end.

"So, what's in Nevada?" the guy asks.

Eddy lets the squeak of the windshield wipers fill the silence for a moment. She wasn't expecting small talk. She hates it under normal circumstances, but tonight it just seems rude.

"Home," she finally says, though that's hardly the truth anymore.

"Huh," he says. "What's behind you, then?"

"Girlfriend," she says. She's deeply familiar with the look that flashes across his face. She almost relishes it. "Ex, actually."

"Oh. Well, I'm sorry."

"It happens."

"You know...everything happens for a reason," he says. "Maybe this is a sign."

"Uh-huh," she says, and counts down the mile markers as he speeds down the highway.

"I need to talk to you," is the first thing that Teresa said when Eddy walked in the next week.

"Well, fuck," Eddy said.

Teresa told her that Matthew knew. Teresa told her that Matthew threatened her. Teresa told her that Matthew was going to tell everyone.

"Fuck him," Eddy said. "Who cares?"

But she knew who cared. She knew Teresa's parents would lose their minds. She knew Teresa's church and school and friends would be horrified and disgusted.

"Not everyone is like your mom, Eddy!" Teresa snapped. "The only reason she doesn't care is because she doesn't care about anything."

Eddy wanted to defend her mother, but Teresa wasn't entirely wrong.

"So that's it?" she said. "You're just going to cow to some shithead nerd's demands?"

And just like that, her bubbly girlfriend was gone and the judgmental bitch she had avoided those first days of camp had reappeared.

"Yes," Teresa said. "Yes, I am. Please get out of my house, Edwina. We're done."

The miles pass. Eddy shifts as she watches the streetlights flicker past.

"That's a wild scar on your hand," she says.

She shouldn't, but she can't help herself and the silence is making her twitchy.

He covers the scar with his other hand, twitching a little. He glances at her quickly in the mirror and then glances away even more quickly. She doesn't think he can see her at all back here thanks to the dark and her hood.

"Uh, yeah," he says. "A misunderstanding with a girl, is all. It's crazy how quickly playing around can trip over into real, you know? Heh."

"I'll bet," Eddy says.

"It's a good, uh, conversation piece," he says. "But mostly I try to downplay it. People can get weird about it."

"Weird about a bite mark on your wrist?" Eddy says dryly. "No kidding."

He forces a laugh and looks at her again in the mirror. She leans back in the seat and goes back to following the mile markers.

It was raining when Eddy got to the highway. No one in town stopped to pick her up, of course—no one in town ever picked her up. Teresa used to drive her to the first rest stop. Sometimes from there she could get a ride nearly all the way home. Without that kind of luck, she was walking through the puddles on the shoulder of the highway with her thumb out.

When a car finally did stop, Eddy almost turned around and went back the other way.

"Edwina!" Matthew shouted after her. "Come on. I'm sorry! You shouldn't have to hitch home in the rain."

Against her better instincts, Eddy sighed and got in the car.

He keeps looking in the mirror, stealing glances at Eddy, though she knows between the dark and the shadows and her hood he can't actually see her.

She counts the mile markers. They're so close.

He gives her a long, lingering look in the mirror and then slams on the breaks.

They skid in the rain.

Eddy flies forward against her seatbelt and her hood falls back. When she sits up again, he's staring at her, mouth dropped open in horror.

"You!" he says.

"Hi, Matthew," Eddy says.

"Gosh, it's coming down like cats and dogs out there," Matthew said, staring out the window. In the passenger seat, Eddy shifted uncomfortably. She was soaked from head to toe, despite her jacket and hood and she still wasn't sure why she got in the car.

"You know," he continued, "I really am sorry about everything that happened."

"I really don't want to talk about this," Eddy muttered. "Can we just drive?"

"It's just, you don't understand. Teresa and I, we have something special."

Eddy pulled at her wet hair. She wasn't one to cry, but it had been a very long day and she could feel the burning creep of tears.

"I really, really don't want to talk about this," she said again.

"We've known each other for years. Our parents were friends through church. We were baptized on the same day. We're just . . . meant to be together."

Eddy ground her teeth together and grabbed the door handle.

"Let me out," she snapped. "Just—let me out of your fucking car, I'll walk back to Nevada."

Matthew looked at her like she was the crazy one. Eyebrows raised, he slowed the car down and pulled onto the shoulder of the road.

"I really am sorry, Edwina," he said. "You seem nice. But you can't get in the way of our future."

"What the fuck—" Eddy started to say, but then Matthew's hands were around her neck.

It took her long, panicked moments to understand what was happening to her. She tried to scream, but she couldn't get enough air. She couldn't even get enough air to breathe, and that panic ripped through her with a surge of adrenaline enough to break his hold by flailing out her elbows. He let go of her throat momentarily and she took in big, heaving lungfuls of air, but he was back on top of her moments later. She clawed out with her fingers, kicked her legs uselessly. When his wrist got close enough, she bit down as hard as she could and he screamed.

"You bitch!" he shouted, and it was enough of a distraction for her to work the door handle and stumble out of the car. He grabbed for her and managed to hook her necklace. For a moment, she couldn't breathe, but then the chain snapped in his hand and she tumbled to the asphalt, scrambling back up. She screamed and screamed again, but the highway was dark and she'd hitched it enough to know there wasn't anyone around for miles. She tried to run and slipped in a puddle, falling back to the ground and scraping her hands and knees. She let out another scream of frustration as she stumbled to her feet.

She managed to make it five more feet before something hit her on the back of the head and everything went dark.

"No!" Matthew shouts. "No, no, no! This is impossible! This is—this *can't be happening!*"

Eddy unbuckles her seatbelt and reaches forward to grab him from behind.

"Fifteen years may seem like a long time, but believe me, it's seemed longer for me," Eddy says, wrapping an arm around his neck. She uses the other to snag her necklace off his mirror. "I'll be taking this back too, you sick fuck."

"I killed you!" Matthew roars before Eddy tightens her grip enough to cut off his airway. He flails uselessly at her, trying to reach around to grab her, trying to pull her arm off of his neck.

"You sure as shit fucking did, you asshole!" she shouts. "And I've been waiting a long time for this!"

He slams on the gas, which she was not expecting, and the car lurches forward. It throws Eddy off, loosens her grip, and then the two of them are pulling and scratching and smacking each other. Eddy grabs his arm and it yanks the wheel all the way to the side. The car squeals off of the road and into the ditch next to it.

It rolls twice and she hears Matthew scream in agony before she blacks out.

Eddy woke up with the sun shining in her eyes.

Except she wasn't in bed. She wasn't lying down at all. She was standing on the side of the road with her thumb sticking out.

She tried to remember if she had been drinking the night before. She tried to remember if she had been smoking anything weird. All she could remember was fighting with Teresa, leaving with Matthew and—shit, Matthew had hit her. Matthew had attacked her.

She must have passed out on the side of the road. Her mother was going to kill her.

She walked down the shoulder until a car finally stopped.

"Where are you headed?" the driver asked. She was a young woman and there were baby toys scattered across the backseat. Of course she was a mom. They were always moms.

"Nevada," Eddy said. "So just the next rest stop is fine."

"I'll take you as far as I can," the woman said. "I hate to see a kid hitching."

Eddy shrugged at her misfortune and got in the back.

It was a long drive. She counted the mile markers until she fell asleep in the backseat.

Eddy woke up with the sun shining in her eyes.

She wasn't in the car. She wasn't in her bed either. She was standing on the side of the road with her thumb out.

"What the fuck," she whispered. "What the fuck. What the *fuck*!"

She looked around, spinning and peering in all directions for anything that might help her figure out what the hell was happening to her. She was half certain she was losing her mind, half certain that someone was going to jump out and tell her she was on *Candid Camera*.

What she did see put everything in stark relief.

What she did see was her body, mangled and bloody, half buried down in the ditch on the side of the road.

"Well," she said. "*Fuck*."

Eddy wakes up with the sun shining in her eyes.

She looks around and curses when she sees the smoldering remains of Matthew's car about fifty yards down the road.

She was so close. It would have been perfect if she had managed to do it in the same exact spot he killed her.

She walks down the shoulder of the road towards the remains of the crash. There are no emergency vehicles, no concerned motorists who have stopped for help.

Good. She'd have been pissed if all of this was for nothing.

She climbs down into the ditch and walks over to the car. The fire is out. What's left of Matthew's corpse is most certainly dead.

It's a pity. She'd have liked to taunt him a little more while she had the chance. She's spent the past fifteen years storing up all manner of invectives she had wanted to unleash on him. But it's over—it's done and she didn't do half bad with what she did manage.

She looks at the wreck and sighs. She doesn't feel transcendently better. She doesn't feel like she's finally at peace. But she can't say she's not grimly satisfied by what's transpired.

She touches her throat and startles for a moment when she feels the cool kiss of a tiny gold star beneath her fingers. Maybe she can keep some nice things after all.

She gives the car one last look and then climbs back up to the shoulder of the road and puts her thumb out, walking slowly down the highway and leaving the crash behind her. She's maybe smiling a little. She's maybe smiling an unsettling amount, but she doubts there will be anyone to see it—no one stops for hitchhikers these days.

in the
backseat

Best Laid Plans

Christine Ricketts

As Matthew drove slowly through the rain, he thought about— Well, he thought about a lot of things. He always did. He was a *thinker*.

But just then he was thinking, as he peered into the gloomy weather, trying to catch sight of that familiar figure, that sometimes you can plan and plan and *plan* and something will *still* come up that you didn't expect.

For instance, he hadn't planned on Eddy. For all the time that he had spent waiting and watching Teresa—following her to school, around school, home from school, around the neighborhood, peering into her bedroom late at night, early in the morning—he hadn't expected Eddy. Just her presence threw everything off balance and that was *before* he even considered her ungodliness.

And so, she had to *go*.

But back to wherever it was that she was from wouldn't be far enough. He hadn't planned for her but now that she was there, smack in the middle of everything, he'd adjust. Even if she went back home and stayed there, far away from him, she might still remember. When he finally finished what he had been planning for so, so, *so* long for Teresa, Eddy might hear about it and remember. Remember him.

That would ruin *everything*. Even more than it had almost already been ruined.

And so, she had to go *all the way* gone.

He just had to find her. She had to be along that stretch of the highway. He knew that she hadn't stayed at Teresa's, knew that Teresa hadn't driven her away like usual. He'd been watching, like always. It had been his intention to go out only a few minutes after he had seen Eddy storm out of the house, just long enough for her to get good and soaked by the rain and disappointment. But then he'd let himself get lost in the anatomy book that he'd been studying to make sure everything else went according to plan. He had lost track of the time and now he was scanning the side of the highway fruitlessly while the gas gauge in his car ran steadily down.

Finally, he was forced to turn off and into an old, rundown station with two badly rusting pumps and a metal shack that might have housed a mini-mart if what you wanted to buy was serial killer paraphernalia. He sniffed at it disdainfully even though there was no one to see. It said "Full Service" on the side of the pumps in peeling yellow paint and he was glad. He wanted to be absolutely *dry* when he found Eddy.

After a few minutes, just as he was considering laying on the horn, a thin man in baggy coveralls wandered out, an oil stained baseball cap tugged down low on his head. Water beaded and dripped from the brim.

Matthew rolled the window down just far enough to hold a crumpled ten dollar bill out. Something about the man's eyes bothered him. They looked at him like . . . like they *knew*. He didn't like the unblinking stare, focused on him. For a moment, completely out of the blue, he wonders if it's how he looks to the girls when he's studying them.

The attendant snatched the bill and lumbered to the back of the car, whistling softly. Matthew didn't know the tune but he didn't like it. The sound of the fuel cap being unscrewed ground out and several seconds later the fuel pump kicked on.

Matthew rolled the window back up, tapping his fingers impatiently against the wheel. He had to find Eddy soon before it got too late. Someone else might pick her up. Someone with better intentions.

A sudden knock on the window made him jump and whip his head to the left. The attendant's face loomed on the other side, dark and blurred by the rain cascading down the glass. Matthew felt his stomach twist and he glanced back over his shoulder at the pump. The numbers were still slowly climbing, the fuel still flowing.

Another knock. He turned back just as the man spoke, his mouth full of broken, jagged teeth.

"Hey. Hey, come outta there." The words were muted, hitting the window and seeming to bounce back. Matthew shook his head, suddenly nervous in a way he had never been before. The knocking continued feverishly until the man stepped back from the car. He turned to reach for something and Matthew decided that he had no interest in seeing what it was. Fumbling with the keys in the ignition, he frantically tried to twist life into the engine. When it finally growled awake, he threw off the brake and slammed on the gas, shooting forward back onto the road in a squeal of tires.

It took nearly ten minutes of driving before his heart calmed to the point that it was no longer pounding in his ears. Ten minutes before he laughed at himself for being so jumpy. Really. What could that attendant have even done to him anyway? Matthew had probably outweighed him by, like, at least ten pounds.

Well. Well, once he had things taken care of with Eddy, and with Teresa, maybe he'd go back and teeth wouldn't be the only broken thing on the attendant's body. He laughed again. It was never too early to start planning.

Something fluttered outside, drawing his attention to the bottom left corner of the windshield. It took him a moment to realize it was a bit of paper stuck in the corner, out of the reach of the wiper. Rolling down the window and leaning forward, he stretched out and grabbed it before it could fly away. The paper was wet and flimsy but the ink scrawled over it had yet to run.

"In the backseat?" he read aloud, frowning to himself. "What the—"

A thin band whipped down in front of his eyes and then there was a pressure against his throat before he could even guess at what was happening.

"Hello, Matthew," Eddy stated to the space just behind his ear. He pawed at his throat with both hands and the car swerved violently. Automatically he dropped one hand back to the wheel to steady it while the fingers of his other tried to find purchase beneath the band that was cutting off his air.

"You know, I'm very annoyed with you Matthew," Eddy continued, wrenching the band tighter, her voice straining slightly. The car began to slow as Matthew took his foot off the gas, trying to shift his weight, to pull back against her grip. To do anything.

He hadn't planned for this.

"I've been watching Teresa for a long time. I've got plans. And I'm not about to let some snot-nosed rat fuck them up."

The car rolled to a stop, gently drifting off the road, as if the driver were merely pulling over for a pause.

Eddy gave the strap a final twist, and then leaned forward to check her handiwork.

Yep, dead as a doornail.

With only a small amount of effort—shit, he really was a puny little punk—she pushed him out of the driver's seat and slid in behind the wheel. There was a turn off not too far up the road that led to a trail and a quiet spot no one would think to look. It wouldn't take long to get him there and then get back.

"Don't worry, you won't be alone for long," Eddy assured the rapidly disinterested Matthew as she checked over her shoulder for oncoming cars. There was nothing but the rain. Putting her blinker on, she drove onto the road and shot him an almost cheery grin.

"I'll be back with Teresa soon."

finally.

Strike
'em Dead.

The Last Ride

Nicole DeGennaro

Eddy can't fucking believe she's still here.

She spends a full few minutes blinking in the sunlight, working through her disbelief. She was certain that getting her revenge on Matthew would let her move on. Why else has she been here for so long? Instead, she's back on the shoulder of the same desert highway she's been hitching on for almost twenty years, and it feels like the first goddamn day after her own death all over again. Disorienting. Lonely. Infuriating.

"Shit," she whispers, and looks around frantically. She must have failed. Matthew must have survived the crash.

She easily spots the smoldering heap of his car, a twisted black skeleton not far off from where he left her body to rot. Even from here she can tell it would be some kind of miracle if he survived. Still, she rushes over to check.

She leans over the wreckage and winces at the sight; it's gruesome even though it also fills her with a grim satisfaction. His body is essentially a charred smudge in a shape that suggests it was once a human.

"Well, this sucks," a familiar voice says from behind her. Eddy spins around. She must be fucking hallucinating, because Matthew is standing there. He's still in his thirties, with graying hair and the hint of some wrinkles lurking around his eyes and mouth. His face has got more punchable with age.

"What the fuck," Eddy breathes. But it's already clear that she's fucked herself.

Matthew is a ghost, just like her.

"This is *bullshit*!" she shouts into the sky. She long ago decided there was no one listening—to prayers or curses—so the yelling is mostly just to make herself feel better. It doesn't work.

She starts to walk away from him, screaming inventive expletives into the desert air. It's not that she had expected any kind of *justice*—that

Matthew's life had been twice as long as hers was proof enough that no such thing existed—but this just wasn't *fair*.

Eddy turns on her heel and stalks back over to Matthew, who recoils. Then he stops, and realization dawns on his face as he understands what Eddy already knows. She can't hurt him—and he can't hurt her either.

"Why the fuck are you here?!" she demands. She doesn't expect an answer from him, because even after all this time, she still doesn't know why *she's* a ghost. It mostly just feels better to be able to direct her frustration at someone else. And this is all his fault, when she boils the situation down to its essence.

"I—I think I—" he stammers. Of course he wouldn't realize it was a rhetorical question.

"Idiot," she spits, and then she's walking away again, this time back up to the shoulder of the road. She needs space, time to think, time to come to terms with the idea that she might be stuck with this asshole for eternity now.

She puts out her thumb and focuses on the horizon, waiting for her next ride.

"Thanks for stopping," Eddy said as she climbed into the backseat of the rusted-out sedan. A strange electric thrill coursed through her as she closed the door and buckled her seatbelt. She hadn't been sure it would work, hitchhiking as a ghost. When the first few cars had passed her by, it had been impossible to tell if they could see her and were ignoring her the way most people ignore a flesh-and-blood hitchhiker, or if she were truly invisible.

"You looked lonely," the old woman said. She smiled at Eddy in the rearview mirror and then put her blinker on to merge with the nonexistent traffic. "I figured we could both use some company. Where can I take you?"

Eddy hadn't thought that far ahead before deciding to try and catch a ride. She wasn't sure she could go anywhere, really. She was still learning the rules, such as they were, of being a ghost.

"Just to the next rest stop is fine, ma'am," she said, her church manners coming out. The elderly woman nodded and sat back in her seat, more relaxed once Eddy proved herself well-behaved. The sun was high overhead; the car seats were probably warm, but Eddy couldn't feel the heat—or anything. But it brought back memories of when she had been alive, and for a time in the back of that sedan she was almost able to forget she had been murdered.

It was a strange sort of comfort, to be able to enjoy an activity in death that she had mostly done out of necessity in life. It helped that there was no longer any risk involved, since she had already gotten into the wrong car once.

She waited for the thought of Matthew to ignite some fire within her, the burning coal of revenge that should power her post-life existence. And sure, she was pissed at him, at the whole situation. But mostly she felt empty. That void, more than anything, was what made her ghostly form insubstantial.

"I haven't seen a hitchhiker in years," the old woman said.

"We're a dying breed," Eddy replied, her gallows humor coming out before she could stop herself. She kept her attention out the window, watching the desert landscape go by as an odd swirl of emotions built up inside her, like a storm rolling in from the horizon. Not quite overhead yet but imminent.

The woman chuckled. "I guess people have stopped trusting one another."

Eddy shifted in her seat, a small noise escaping her as her unease mounted. There was no physical sensation to it, which made it more disconcerting. It was more like her incorporeal form had suddenly become home to every emotion she had ever experienced, all of it washing over her like a driving rain. She hadn't experienced anything like it since becoming a ghost, but instead of being alarmed she was mostly surprised. Between the waves of elation and despair and fury and embarrassment and boredom and lust and disgust.

"Are you all right?" the woman asked, and the car began to slow. Eddy made eye contact in the rearview mirror and the woman shouted in surprise before jerking her car onto the shoulder. The rumble strip jostled the vehicle, but Eddy hardly noticed, still struggling to piece together what the hell was going on.

Then, as quickly as it came on, the emotions began to recede. Confused, Eddy glanced down to see her hand disappearing, followed swiftly by the rest of her.

"Sorry," she said to the woman, understanding the panic on her face. By the time the car came to a stop, Eddy was gone.

"Why do you do that?" Matthew asks her. She had hoped he would be smart enough not to fucking bother her, but apparently wisdom only comes with age for certain people. She's moving down the shoulder, thumb out, trying to hitch another ride because it's the only chance she has now for some time to herself.

"I mean, you know you're just going to end up back here. So why bother?"

And most of the drivers are *way* less chatty than Matthew. He just has a constant need to *explain* and *analyze* and be a goddamned know-it-all. And when she doesn't answer, he just *keeps talking* as if she had.

If she could kill him again, she would. And it still wouldn't be close to everything he deserves.

She levels her gaze at him. "It gets me the fuck away from you."

"I'm only here because of *you*," he says, an edge to his voice that Eddy almost welcomes. She comes to a stop on the shoulder, drops her thumb. Then she laughs. When a flash of anger crosses Matthew's face, she laughs harder.

"Sure, Matthew. *I'm* the reason you're here. You've got this whole situation all figured out."

"I know more about it than you do!" he shouts, and even though he appears to be in his thirties, he sounds like a toddler. She half expects him to stomp his foot and pout.

"Right. Just like you knew what was best for Teresa, huh? Nice to see death hasn't humbled you at all, you fucking prick." Eddy sticks her thumb out again, still holding Matthew's gaze. So she sees his anger crack apart, watches uncertainty flicker in his eyes. She can't believe *this* is the person who killed her, that she ever thought he had anything to do with why she was a ghost. He's pathetic.

"You ruined everything," he mutters as he looks away from her unwavering gaze.

"Jesus *Christ*," she hisses, moving toward him. "You *murdered me*, but *I'm* the one that ruined everything?"

Without thinking, she reaches out and shoves him. To both their surprise, he stumbles backward. Eddy doesn't think she actually made contact, but there was still a push, like the force of her will repelled him. But she doesn't revel in the terror that contorts Matthew's face. Instead, she stops.

It's not so much his fear, or the idea that maybe she can still hurt him, that startles her. It's the raw anger she feels, something she never experienced while alive—something that might be impossible for the living to really know. Without a corporeal form, there are no physical sensations. What makes up Eddy now is almost entirely her consciousness and energy, so she can still experience emotions. But because that's all she can feel, they're more potent, like they've been distilled to their purest form.

The only time she usually feels something like that is in the cars, right before she vanishes. It's like her life flashing before her eyes again but instead it's just the emotions in a rapid flurry, overlapping and overwhelming, each intense but short.

This is different, because it's just the one feeling. With no other emotions waiting in the wings to usher it out of the spotlight, the anger takes her over completely. It wants her to keep going after Matthew, to tear him apart with the force of her rage.

It's tempting, so tempting, but she also sees the specter of something dark lurking in there. So she pulls herself back from it before she can be consumed.

It didn't take Eddy long to figure out she was a ghost. But she did struggle to figure out *why*. All she knew about ghosts were stories she had heard while she was alive. Ghosts wanted revenge, justice. They wanted the truth to be known, or they didn't realize they were dead. They wanted to atone for some terrible deed. Or they were so warped they simply wanted to cause pain to the living.

Point was, ghosts existed for a *reason*. It seemed to her that the reason would be what created the ghost, an immense act of willpower that bucked the natural order of things in those last few moments of life. A singular focus on any unfinished business.

Eddy had certainly been willful while she had been alive, and she doubted that it had changed in death. But if she were honest, her last moments were mostly spent panicked and afraid. She hadn't used her dying breath to curse Matthew or swear revenge. But she had become a ghost anyway.

At first, she continued to hitchhike because she didn't know what else to do. Maybe she'd somehow figure out more about her purpose by riding the same five-mile stretch of road over and over again. It certainly gave her time to think, and it was better than just standing near the place where Matthew had hidden her body.

It was when she was in the back of a station wagon, wedged between two empty car seats, that her first potential purpose struck her. The man driving had put on a classic rock station and was tapping a finger to the beat on the steering wheel. It was a dark, clear night, the desert reflecting the moonlight and glittering like broken glass.

"You don't look well," the man said. Eddy was used to hearing that by now. She knew that when she started to feel the emotions swirling, she would start to disappear shortly after. It happened in subtle ways first, like the edges of her form becoming less defined. Which was hard for the drivers to process, because they thought she was flesh and blood like they were. So they tended to translate it the only way they could—by thinking she was carsick.

Eddy lurched forward and clutched the man's shoulder. He yelped and the car swerved for a moment before he regained composure.

"Help me," Eddy said, meeting his gaze. "I'm stuck here."

The man kept driving after she vanished. But she was there a few days later when someone from the sheriff's department found her body. Whether the man had sent them or it had been a coincidence, she never figured out.

All she knew was that even after they took what remained of her body away, which thanks to scavengers by that point was maybe about half the number of bones that typically composed a human body, she stayed behind.

Still confined to the highway. Still a ghost. Still without a purpose.

When she reappears after her latest ride, she's somewhat surprised to see Matthew standing on the shoulder, watching the horizon. He hasn't noticed she's returned, so she stays down in the ditch watching him. Maybe some of what she said to him during their fight finally sank in.

That faint phantom of hope vanishes the minute a car approaches and Matthew starts flailing and yelling at it. Predictably, it speeds by without even a flicker of the tail lights. Eddy sighs, which alerts Matthew to her presence. He scowls at her.

"They aren't going to stop if you wave your arms like an asshole," Eddy says, although she suspects there's another reason they aren't stopping.

He turns back to the road, and she walks up to join him out in the open. Another car is approaching, still a little ways off. At first Eddy wonders if the car that sped by Matthew just before has turned around, but as this one comes into clearer view, it's an SUV, not a sedan.

"Hey!" Matthew yells as it approaches. He steps into the road, since the car is on the other side, and waves at it. "Hey, there's been an accident!" He waves and then motions to the ditch, where his car is hidden from the view of passing vehicles. Eddy keeps herself from being seen, and the SUV also continues on its way.

"I told you," she says when Matthew drops his arms and watches the vehicle vanish into the distance. "I've been here fifteen years *and* I hitched more than you while I was alive. I know what I'm talking about."

"That's exactly why I'm *not* listening to you," he snaps. "You've been here *fifteen fucking years*." He keeps his distance, though, she notices with a bit of satisfaction. "I'm not trying to hitch a useless ride to nowhere to pass the time. I'm trying to move on." He keeps his attention on the road, although there's not even the mirage of a car on the horizon.

As much as she's able to shrug off most of his bullshit, this time his words sting. She clenches her fists and forces herself not to lash out at him like she did before. Even if it might make her feel better. She's worried that if she gives into that anger one too many times, she won't be able to come back from it. And then whatever hope she has of someday being able to move on would really be gone.

Because that's what got her, about what Matthew said. His implication that she hasn't been fucking trying to move on this whole time, that she was just waiting for him to drive down this road again. She'd always known he was a self-absorbed asshole, but it's worse than she thought, especially now that she's stuck with him.

"And what exactly is your master plan, Matthew?" she asks, walking around him until she's in his line of sight again. His car is in the ditch right behind her, and his gaze doesn't know where to go, so he keeps glancing from her to just past her. Then back again. She pauses longer than she intended, letting him squirm. "Wave down a car and point them at the wreck? Good luck, dipshit."

His eyes have settled on her, and she sees the same hate there that she feels for him. Maybe she should be the bigger person—or ghost—and forgive him, but she just doesn't have it in her. Some people are beyond forgiveness.

"Is this just how you're going to be for as long as we're both here?" he asks. The vitriol has leaked out of him, leaving his voice small and exhausted. "A foul-mouthed asshole know-it-all?"

"Hey, don't talk about yourself like that," she replies with a smirk. His mouth opens and closes as he flounders for a comeback. "Yes, this is how I'm going to be. You've always been a dick *and* a killer, and you *really* think the reason you're stuck here is no one has found your worthless corpse?"

"It's the reason *you're* still here!" he shouts, and he rushes toward her. There's a brief wave of something that passes over her, maybe him trying to impose his will on her. But it's not strong enough, and so he stops short when she doesn't budge.

Eddy opens her mouth with a scathing rebuttal, but it lodges in her throat, and she can almost taste the truth of it.

Everything shifts around her. The sand looks less like a tan mass and more like thousands of shades of brown and yellow. The clouds become the purest white she's ever seen. The air that seemed so silent before carries the sounds of distant desert birdsong to her ears.

"Newsflash," Eddy says as she comes back to herself, but different than she was before. She crosses the street, because over Matthew's shoulder she's caught the familiar glint of a windshield reflecting sunlight. "They found my fucking worthless corpse."

He stares at her, stunned, as she sticks her thumb out. For a moment he looks gaunt, and she can only guess what's going through his mind. Disbelief that her remains were found but he didn't get tied to her murder? Or maybe he's finally started having the post-life existential crisis that she's been dealing with for over a decade.

As the minivan pulls onto the shoulder for her, she decides she doesn't fucking care what's happening with Matthew. She has better things to do. So when she turns to close the car door behind her, she flips him the bird.

Eddy cycled through a few more ideas of what her purpose might be before settling on revenge. It happened during a ride with two friends road tripping across the country. They pulled over, offered her a cigarette, then told her how this was their last hurrah before college. They kept glancing at one another, a mixture of sadness and excitement on their faces. Eddy was pretty sure the driver had a crush on the passenger.

"Are you two going to the same college?" Eddy asked. The brief moment of silence told her everything she needed to know.

"No—uh, she's smarter than me, got accepted into a *way* better school," the girl driving said. Eddy kept thinking of her as a *girl* even though she was probably older than Eddy had ever lived to be, even if only by a year or two. The passenger blushed and slapped her friend's shoulder in a playful way.

"*Stop*," she muttered with a small smile. Maybe Eddy was wrong—maybe they both had a crush on one another. "But we promised we'd still talk all the time."

Eddy nodded, but there was something else building up in her beyond the familiar emotions as they approached the mile marker that she wouldn't be able to pass. She probably wouldn't have gone to university if she hadn't been killed, anyway. Wouldn't have been able to afford even a few classes at the local community college.

And she doubted she and Teresa would have stayed together for more than maybe a couple of years. But she would have liked the chance to see if she was wrong. Maybe she could have gotten a scholarship, or Teresa would have come out to her parents, Eddy by her side.

That was the kicker, wasn't it? Things *changed*. Life could take a turn when you least expected it. And Matthew had robbed her of the chance to see how hers would play out.

"Thank you," she said to the two friends as she began to vanish. She kept her eyes closed tight, not wanting to see the girls' shock and horror as she dissipated. She wanted to remember the sideways glances they stole at one another. She wanted to remember the possibilities of their lives still stretching out ahead of them.

That was when she decided that if she ever got the opportunity, she would take in kind what Matthew had taken from her.

When she reappeared, it was nighttime. The sky stretched endlessly overhead, millions of stars hanging above her. The moon was dark that night, and Eddy stood staring, waiting. She waited for the sense of satisfaction to wash over her. To make her less of a hollow in the shape of a dead teenage girl.

She waited all night, but it never came. Eventually she crossed the street and stuck her thumb out even though the only lights were from the stars. Revenge *had* to be her purpose, because if it wasn't, she didn't know what else could be. She hadn't really had any expectations of the afterlife or whatever this was, but if she had given it some thought, she would not have expected so much uncertainty. Everything should have been clearer now that there were fewer things for her to worry about.

But with all the trappings of mortality having fallen away, it meant nothing could distract her from the one thing bothering her. Because coming to a decision about the purpose of her existence as a ghost was not the same as finding the driving force, the thing anchoring her to the living.

It was funny, really, if she were honest. She had never worried about the *why* of her existence when she was alive because it had always been clear to her that there wasn't a purpose. And it never bothered her. She enjoyed herself without worrying about any "plan" that God or the universe or whatever had for her.

But she couldn't shake the feeling that there should have been a reason for her being a ghost. Because if there wasn't, she was potentially staring down the barrel of an eternity hitchhiking the same stretch of road. It meant there was nothing for her to *do* that would then allow her to move on. It would mean she was just here, and what would happen to her when there was no *here* anymore? Would she still be a ghost, a void haunting a bigger void?

"Christ, pull it together, Edwina," she muttered to herself. The sound of her voice against all the emptiness did help halt the cyclical thoughts.

Maybe getting revenge on Matthew wasn't her ultimate purpose, but it at least gave her something concrete to focus on between rides.

She takes a few trips before enacting her plan, just to let Matthew keep failing in his shitty scheme. It also gives her some time to reflect.

Eddy doesn't know how many years it was after she died when she finally decided she'd get her revenge on Matthew if she ever got a chance. Time doesn't work the same for ghosts because it doesn't matter as much. And it's essentially impossible for her to tell how much time passes between when she disappears from a car and reappears on the shoulder.

She certainly hadn't been expecting it to be fifteen years before she'd get the opportunity for revenge. In some ways, it felt like the blink of an eye. In others, it felt like eternity. In those years, she had reasoned with herself that if there was no purpose to life, there wouldn't be a purpose to the afterlife, either. Everything she knew about what happened in death was from a bunch of stories the living told one another. Nobody alive actually knew what being dead was like, just like they didn't know shit about ghosts either.

It was not an easy revelation to have, and she only realized after Matthew's ghost had joined her roadside existence had she had never accepted it. A part of her had still clung to the hope that if she did get her revenge, it would solve the last of her problems and she would finally, *finally* move on. As time had dragged on and blinked by, she had fooled herself into thinking that realizing something and believing something were the same.

But they weren't, and the acceptance that she had no purpose had only truly come during her last fight with Matthew. She had nearly yelled at him *There is no reason! You're just fucking stuck here, like me.* But the words hit her instead, really settled deep, like sediment in water. Her mind had been clouded by this idea of purpose for so long that she had forgotten what clarity looked like. For the first time she could remember as a ghost, she *felt* something, a real physical sensation, and it was the weight of reality.

With that feeling came something else, a sort of sliver of light she could only see in her peripheral vision. Like the universe had opened a door for her. Like she had finally found the key. Even now, in this car, she can see it hovering there at the corner of her eye. Ready for her to turn toward it with her whole self. But, she finds, she has one more thing she wants to do.

"You all right, Eddy?" the driver, Jamie, asks. She had told them her real name when they asked earlier. She usually didn't do that, but everything is different now. She knows this is her last ride, and maybe she wants to pretend she has a friend. Someone who knows her real name, someone who might remember her. She's relieved that she can move on, but there's also a small part of her that's afraid.

She shifts in her seat, meets their eyes in the rearview mirror and gives a small smile.

"Yeah, sorry. Just a lot of memories on this stretch of road."

"I can't believe you hitchhike out here all the time. It's so desolate."

"There's a lot more going on here than you think."

They're traveling in the opposite direction than usual, toward the place where Eddy and Matthew died instead of away from it. As the car approaches, Matthew is waving like a lunatic at it, until he sees Eddy peering out the back window. His mouth falls open in shock. From Jamie's complete lack of reaction, Eddy knows her suspicions were right—the living can't see Matthew. Not yet, anyway. Maybe because it hasn't occurred to him that he has to will himself into being visible. Matthew never had that strength of personality like Eddy.

She sits up straighter, pretending she just noticed something. "Hey, Jamie. I think I saw something in the ditch over there."

"What, really? Out here?" Jaime slows but seems uncertain.

"Maybe someone crashed."

At that, Jaime eases the car onto the shoulder and reverses until Eddy points.

"There, see?"

They put the car in park and crane their neck over the passenger seat.

"Oh shit." They turn off the car and scramble out. Eddy moves more slowly, climbing out of the car and shadowing Jaime as they ease their way down into the ditch, where Matthew's car sits overturned and burned out. She turns away to look at Matthew, who is still standing on the shoulder, agape.

"I'm going to call 9-1-1!" Jaime yells up from the wreck. Eddy locks eyes with Matthew.

"Good idea," she replies. Matthew's look of surprise shifts to one of confusion and then, oddly, panic. A wave of satisfaction floods Eddy, and she smirks at him.

"What the hell is going on, Edwina?!" he yells as he runs toward her.

Jaime climbs back up to the shoulder, looking a little green in the face.

"It's gruesome," they mutter as they hang up the phone. "But whoever they were, seems like they were alone."

Matthew has reached Eddy, although he's still invisible to Jaime. Eddy hardly notices either of them. The weight that settled on her before is now drawing her to the door. Heaviness always has a negative connotation, but it has been a relief to Eddy. She had been weightless, aimless for so long, skirting the edge of that cold, looming void that would have happily sucked her in at any moment and warped her into the darkest version of herself.

To feel grounded again is a boon.

The door opens a little wider, and the space beyond it is warm and inviting and feels more like *home* than anything in the past fifteen years.

"EDWINA!" Matthew shouts. Eddy looks down to see that she's disappearing.

"Eddy?" Jaime asks, their fear almost tangible. She smiles at them.

"It's okay," she says. "I've been waiting for this for a long time."

She turns toward the doorway, placing it in the center of her mind, and flips Matthew the bird one last time. She hopes he never fucking figures it out.

And then, she's gone.

In the Air

Lara Eckener

The girl gives up her hair, girl gives up her voice,
girl gives up her body when she gives up on love,

and in so doing becomes the air, becomes the sea froth
lighter than the air, becomes the absence of a girl

in a bed chamber where the only blood drawn has already
dried on the sheets, and this empty space is her reward,

for never once has a blade cut through the wind
and exposed the inside of it, drawn forth rivulets

of purple and red and gold, the blush at the edges
of the night sky, she will lose track of this agony,

because the air is humid with agonies, striking
each other, erupting into lightning, buffeted and

condensed into rain, and eventually her beloved will forget
she was ever there, but will not be able to ignore that

the rain clings so much more heavily than it did in
their youth, that sometimes sweat rolls up their backs

instead of down, that though they did not drown at sea
there are things to drown in besides water, even though

the majority of men drown in their own years, every one
of them reaches for heaven in the end, forgetting

that anyone who might save them long ago left behind
the skin and skirts of humanity, leaving them

begging for mercy that will not be granted a second time.

Behind the Tales

Have I mentioned that I love mythology?

Ok, good. Just checking.

Anyway, I asked Nicole, Lara, and Kaitlyn to talk a little bit about what inspired their original entries in the collection. If you know them as well as I do, you won't be surprised at all by their choices but I guarentee you'll be fascinated by their answers.

Because why does anyone tell a story? To teach, to inspire, to terrify, to unlock the metaphysical mysteries of the universe?

Sometimes just because the story is there, begging to be told. And one of the very best things about being a writer is reaching out, taking hold of it, and shaping it as best you can as you put it down on the page. If you're lucky, it can shape you back, helping you grow and bringing you joy.

And if you're really lucky, it helps shape someone else.

The myth of Orpheus and Eurydice has always been one of my favorites within any mythology. When I was younger, I thought it was sad and heartbreaking, the way Orpheus voyages all the way through Hades, traverses all the dangers of the Underworld, charms Hades himself to save his love only to loose her again at the very last second. It was romantic to think of a lover willing to traverse Hell in order to rescue their beloved.

As I've gotten older, my thoughts on death and loss have evolved, as I think everyone's do. I've experienced two personal losses within eight years, nearly to the day. Part of me wishes for the chance to undertake some journey, regardless of the cost, that could potentially bring those people back to me. Or even just afford me a few more precious moments in their company. But a larger part understands that despite the desperate wish there is no way to go back. I think one of the things that loss cements within us is the painful fact time truly only flows in one direction. You can only ever go forward.

With this version of the myth, I wanted to focus on the aspect of loss that feels the most insidious. Time. How even in the face of the most obvious signs telling us otherwise, we can always think we have plenty of it. There is so much that grabs Owen's attention, some friviolous, some achingly important, that you can't really blame him from wandering. When things have been a part of your life for so long, have been so steady and comforting, it can be hard to remember to reach for them. Until it's too late.

Don't wait.

Our lives are made up of a million myths. Some were told to us, passed down by family or society or history. Some we tell ourselves, as a coping mechanism or a comfort or a challenge. They can be big or small, conscious or subconscious. But they are all dangerous if we never question them.

The idea of questioning myths is a centerpiece of all my stories in this collection. No matter the size of the central myth, there is always something in the main conceit that doesn't hold up to scrutiny. Sometimes this shifts a character's perspective of themselves; sometimes it shifts their perspective of their society or surroundings.

Specifically, *The Hag's Hand* is a confluence of this idea with several others that have been fermenting in my brain: who controls the narrative of any given story; the #ownvoices and We Need Diverse Books movements, which highlight the power of people being able to tell their own stories; and women and magic.

I also took some guidance from the masterful work of one of my favorite writers, Ursula K. Le Guin. She often lays out her worlds with such depth and detail that you are enthralled—and then she pulls the rug out from under you (and often the narrator). Most of her stories revolve around challenging the rules and tenets of the very world she created.

All of this is how *The Hag's Hand* came to be. The beginning narrative is created and controlled by the male-dominant society in which Ellie lives: hags and their magic are evil and to be feared. Thom is a fervent believer of this myth, whereas Pa has his secret doubts after it was used against Ma. Ellie is kept in ignorance and has to learn for herself that the myth of the hag's hand and women's magic is entirely false. The hags, and Ellie, begin to take control of the narrative and reveal that their magic, instead of being evil, is literally lifesaving.

When you create space for people to tell their own stories, as Ellie does with the hags, you might be surprised by how much of what you thought you knew is false. This is something I'm trying to become more aware of in my life and in society at large. There is value in absorbing other people's personal stories—through whatever medium they choose—and examining your feelings and reactions. Question your myths, and who told them to you and why.

This is always a work in progress, the work of a lifetime, especially if you are part of the group that has been controlling the narrative for centuries. But it is some of the only work worth doing. Don't be a Thom. Be an Ellie.

Be a hag.

I chose oracles as the subject for my main poem in this collection because they embody two mythic things I can never quite reconcile: time and religion. I find it impossible to sit in a church or a graveyard or a concert venue or next to a statue in a park and not think about all of the people who have been there before me—worshipping, wanting. What did the future look like to them? Did they think about how they were pulling it down around themselves breath by breath?

In the myths, heroes seek out oracles in moments of desperation or desire. An oracle's work is to shine light ahead on a path that those of us sitting in pews or stretched out in the grass wish desperately to see to the end. They have been touched by the divine and gifted with fragments of a future that no one—not even if every oracle placed their predictions end to end—will see in its entirety. We forget that oracles are human too. That they're warm. That these fragments madden them. That they too breathe in the future and breathe out the past, one breath after another, until they reach the place where darkness reclaims the path.

I can't remember when or how I discovered the first shelf in the non-fiction section in the library, sparse and tucked into the corner. I know I was small—it was at some point during elementary school—but I don't have a clear memory of being brought there by a librarian or stumbling over it myself. What I do vividly remember is making a beeline to that corner in my school library on every single visit. I remember looking over the spines of the books on those first few shelves, the ones that contained the 000s and the 130s, and pulling out my favorites. If you opened the front cover of most of them, my name would be the only one on check-out card for the past three, four, sometimes five loans.

In those sections, the sections on aliens and cryptids and the occult, I would read book after book of ghost stories, monster stories, UFO stories. "Real" stories—not the fiction in the books like *Scary Stories to Tell in the Dark* and the *Point Horror* collections that lined my shelves at home and that made up my other library loans, but non-fiction. Things that (supposedly) actually happened.

Despite that, there was a rhythm to these stories, a repetition. You could pick five different books about American ghost stories at random and see the same tales repeated with slightly different details—the man who stops to pick up a hitchhiker only for the young woman to disappear when he arrives at her requested destination, the couple at lover's lane who hear about the escaped murderer with a hook for a hand who is lurking in the woods, the lights in the sky that precede a visit from small grey creatures who speak straight into your mind, the graverobber who steals from the recently deceased and then wakes in the middle of the night to a spectral visitor demanding their property be returned.

They're stories that everyone knows, picked up from sleepovers and campfires, television and movies. They're woven into the American mythos, familiar enough that I can reference them in just a few words and the whole of the story, as you first heard it, will materialize in your mind. At their core, these stories serve practical purposes: warnings against traveling alone at night or wandering from the path in the woods, reminders about trusting strangers or desecrating the dead. Taken together, they also provide a reflection of our lives and cultural values, a snapshot of life in America at various points in time. Every ghost, every cryptid, every supernatural encounter is grown from a kernel of fear, some of them unique to the varied and sprawling landscape of the United States.

But not all of them. The nature of this project presented me with three stories created by others from their own favored mythos. Finding a through-line to my passion, these spooky encounters and cautionary tales carved out of America's cultural fears, was more difficult than I expected. In the end, however, many of these fears are transitive. Across countries and cultures we've always been afraid of things beyond our understanding or things we find threatening, whether it be women with too much power or people who can see the future or the passage of time or meeting a stranger on a dark road.

The stories in this collection may seem familiar, may take you back to stories you've read or movies you've watched or podcasts you've listened to. It's possible, though, that familiarity comes from somewhere deeper. We've all been alone on a dark road in the quiet of the night. We've all found ourselves lost on a journey and afraid we'd never reach our destination. We've all been confronted with a truth that we are unable to make others understand.

Some fears are universal. Lean into those fears—they're universal for a reason.

www.ingramcontent.com/pod-product-compliance
Lightning Source LLC
Chambersburg PA
CBHW051516030726
47592CB00006B/2298